TIN MAN

ALSO BY SARAH WINMAN

When God Was a Rabbit

A Year of Marvellous Ways

TIN MAN

Sarah Winman

VIKING

VIKING

an imprint of Penguin Canada, a division of Penguin Random House Canada Limited

Canada • USA • UK • Ireland • Australia • New Zealand • India • South Africa • China

First published in Great Britain in 2017 by Tinder Press, an imprint of Headline Publishing Group
Published in Viking paperback by Penguin Canada, 2018
Simultaneously published in the United States by G. P. Putnam's Sons, an imprint of
Penguin Random House (LLC)

www.penguinrandomhouse.ca

*Publisher's note: This book is a work of fiction. Names, characters, places and incidents either
are the product of the author's imagination or are used fictitiously, and any resemblance
to actual persons living or dead, events, or locales is entirely coincidental.*

LIBRARY AND ARCHIVES CANADA CATALOGUING IN PUBLICATION

Winman, Sarah, author
Tin man / Sarah Winman.

Issued in print and electronic formats.
ISBN 978-0-7352-3515-1 (softcover).—ISBN 978-0-7352-3516-8 (electronic)

I. Title.

PR6123.I62T56 2018   823'.92   C2017-907156-4
                                             C2017-907157-2

Book design by Meighan Cavanaugh
Interior image: (sunflower) inspiring/Shutterstock.com
Cover design by Grace Han
Cover images: Sunflowers, 1888 (oil on canvas), Gogh, Vincent van (1853-90) / Neue
Pinakothek, Munich, Germany / Bridgeman Images;
(waves) Nata Alhontess/Shutterstock.com

Printed and bound in the United States of America

10 9 8 7 6 5 4 3 2 1

Penguin
Random House
VIKING CANADA

For Robert Caskie
and for Patsy

I already feel that it has done me good to go South,
the better to see the North.

Vincent van Gogh in a letter to
his brother Theo, May 1890

1950

All Dora Judd ever told anyone about that night three weeks before Christmas was that she won the painting in a raffle.

She remembered being out in the back garden, as lights from the Cowley Car Plant spilled across the darkening sky, smoking her last cigarette, thinking there must be more to life.

Back inside, her husband said, Bloody move it, will you, and she said, Give it a rest, Len, and she began to undo her housedress as she made her way upstairs. In the bedroom, she looked at herself sideways in the mirror, her hands feeling for the progression of her pregnancy, this new life she knew was a son.

She sat down at her dressing table and rested her chin on her hands. She thought her eyes looked tired, her skin dry.

She painted her lips red and the color instantly lifted her face. It did little for her mood, however.

The moment she walked through the door of the Community Center, she knew it had been a mistake to come. The room was smoky and festive drinkers jostled as they tried to get to the bar. She followed her husband through the crowds and the intermittent wafts of perfume and hair oil, bodies and beer.

She wasn't up for socializing with him anymore, not the way he behaved with his friends, making a point of looking at every pretty thing that passed, making sure she was watching. She stood off to the side holding a glass of warm orange juice that was beginning to make her feel sick. Thank God Mrs. Powys made a beeline for her, clutching a book of raffle tickets.

Top prize was a bottle of Scotch whisky, said Mrs. Powys, as she took Dora over to the table where the prizes were laid out. Then we have a radio, a voucher for a haircut and set at Audrey's Coiffure, a tin of Quality Street sweets, a pewter hip flask, and lastly—and she leaned forward for this confidence—a midsize oil painting of very little worth. Albeit a fine copy of a European work of art, she added with a wink.

Dora had seen the original on a school trip to London at the National Gallery's Pimlico site. Fifteen years old she'd been, full of the contradictions of that age. But when she had entered the gallery room, the storm shutters around her heart flew open and she knew immediately that this was the life she wanted: Freedom. Possibility. *Beauty.*

There were other paintings in the room, too, she remembered—van Gogh's *Chair* and Seurat's *Bathers at Asnières*—but it was as if she had fallen under this particular painting's spell, and whatever had transfixed her then, and drawn her into the inescapable confines of its frame, was exactly what was pleading with her now.

Mrs. Judd? said Mrs. Powys.

Mrs. Judd? repeated Mrs. Powys. Can I tempt you to a ticket, then?

What?

A raffle ticket?

Oh, yes. Of course.

THE LIGHTS FLICKERED on and off and a man tapped a spoon against a glass. The room quietened as Mrs. Powys made a great show of reaching into the cardboard box and pulling out the first winning ticket. Number seventeen, she said, grandly.

Dora was too distracted by the feelings of nausea to hear Mrs. Powys, and it was only when the woman next to

her nudged her and said, It's you! that Dora realized she
had won. She held up her ticket and said, I'm seventeen!
and Mrs. Powys shouted, It's Mrs. Judd! Mrs. Judd is our
first winner! and led her over to the table to take her pick
of the prizes.

Leonard shouted out for her to choose the whisky.

Mrs. Judd? said Mrs. Powys, quietly.

But Dora said nothing, she stared at the table.

Get the whisky, Leonard shouted again. The whisky!
And slowly, in unison, the men's voices chanted, Whisky!
Whisky! Whisky!

Mrs. Judd? said Mrs. Powys. Will it be the whisky?
And Dora turned and faced her husband and said, No,
I don't like whisky. I choose the painting instead.

It was her first ever act of defiance. Like cutting off an
ear. And she made it in public.

She and Len left shortly after. They sat separately on
the bus journey home, her up, him down. When they got
off, he stormed ahead of her, and she fell back into the
peace of her star-aligned night.

The front door was ajar when she arrived and the house
was dark, no noise from upstairs. She went quietly into the
back room and turned on the light. It was a drab room,
furnished by one pay packet, his. Two armchairs were set
by the hearth and a large dining table that had witnessed

little conversation over the years blocked the way to the kitchen. There was nothing on those brown walls except a mirror, and Dora knew she should hang the painting in the shadow of the dresser away from his sight, but she couldn't help herself, not that night. And she knew if she didn't do it then, she never would. She went to the kitchen and opened his toolbox. She took out a hammer and a nail and came back to the wall. A few gentle taps and the nail moved softly and easily into the plaster.

She stood back. The painting was as conspicuous as a newly installed window, but one that looked out onto a life of color and imagination, far away from the gray factory dawn and in stark contrast to the brown curtains and brown carpet, both chosen by a man to hide the dirt.

It would be as if the sun itself rose every morning on that wall, showering the silence of their mealtimes with the shifting emotion of light.

The door exploded and nearly came off its hinges. Leonard Judd made a lunge for the painting, and as quickly as she had ever moved in her life, Dora stood in front of it, raised the hammer, and said, Do it and I'll kill you. If not now, then when you sleep. This painting is me. You don't touch it, you respect it. Tonight I'll move into the spare room. And tomorrow you'll buy yourself another hammer.

All for a painting of sunflowers.

ELLIS

1996

In the front bedroom, propped up among the books, is a color photograph of three people, a woman and two men. They are tightly framed, their arms around one another, and the world beyond is out of focus, and the world on either side excluded. They look happy, they really do. Not just because they are smiling but because there is something in their eyes, an ease, a joy, something they share. It was taken in spring or summer, you can tell by the clothes they are wearing (T-shirts, pale colors, that sort of thing), and, of course, because of the light.

One of the men from the photograph, the one in the middle with scruffy dark hair and kind eyes, is asleep in that room. His name is Ellis. Ellis Judd. The photograph, there among the books, is barely noticeable, unless you know where to find it, and because Ellis no longer has any desire to read, there is little compulsion for him to move toward the photograph, and for him to pick it up and to reminisce about the day, that spring or summer day, on which it was taken.

THE ALARM CLOCK went off at five in the afternoon as it always did. Ellis opened his eyes and turned instinctively to the pillow next to him. Through the window dusk had fallen. It was February still, the shortest month, which never seemed to end. He got up and turned off the alarm. He continued across the landing to the bathroom and stood over the toilet bowl. He leaned a hand against the wall and began to empty his bladder. He didn't need to lean against the wall anymore but it was the unconscious act of a man who had once needed support. He turned the shower on and waited until the water began to steam.

Washed and dressed, he went downstairs and checked the time. The clock was an hour fast because he had forgotten to put it back last October. However, he knew that in a month the clocks would go forward and the problem would right itself. The phone rang as it always did, and he picked it up and said, Carol. Yes, I'm all right. OK then. You, too.

He lit the stove and brought two eggs to the boil. Eggs

were something he liked. His father did, too. Eggs were where they came together in agreement and reconciliation.

He wheeled his bike out into the freezing night and cycled down Divinity Road. At Cowley Road he waited for a break in the traffic heading east. He had done this journey thousands of times and could close his mind and ride at one with the black tide. He turned into the sprawling lights of the Car Plant and headed over to the Paint Shop. He was forty-five years old, and every night he wondered where the years had gone.

The stink of white spirit caught in his throat as he walked across the line. He nodded to men he had once socialized with, and in the Tinny Bay, he opened his locker and took out a bag of tools. Garvy's tools. Every one of them handmade, designed to get behind a dent and to knock it out. People reckoned he was so skilled at it he could take the cleft out of a chin without the face knowing. Garvy had taught him everything. First day with him, Garvy picked up a file and struck a discarded door panel and told him to get the dent out.

Keep your hand flat, he'd said. Like this. Learn to feel the dent. Look with your hands, not your eyes. Move across it gently. Feel it. Stroke it. Gently now. Find the pimple. And he stood back, all downward mouth and critical eye.

Ellis picked up the dolly, placed it behind the dent and began to tap above with the spoon. He was a natural.

Listen to the sound! Garvy'd shouted. Get used to the sound. The ringing lets you know if you've spotted it right. And when Ellis had finished, he stood up pleased with himself because the panel was as smooth as if it had just been pressed. Garvy said, Reckon it's out, do you?

And Ellis said, Course I do. And Garvy closed his eyes and ran his hands across the seam and said, Not out.

They used to listen to music back then, but only once Ellis knew the sound that metal made. Garvy liked Abba, he liked the blonde one best, Agnetha someone, but he never told anyone else. Over time, though, Ellis came to realize the man was so lonely and eager for companionship that the process of smoothing out a dent was as if his hands were running across a woman's body.

Later in the canteen, the others would stand behind him and pout, run their hands down their make-believe breasts and waists, and they would whisper, Close your eyes, Ellis. Do you feel it, that slight pimple? Can you feel it, Ellis? Can you?

It was Garvy, who sent him to the trim shop to ask for a "trim woman," the silly sod, but only the once, mind. And when he retired, Garvy said, Take two things from me,

Ellis boy. First—work hard and you'll have a long life here. And second—my tools.

Ellis took the tools.

Garvy died a year after retiring. This place had been his oxygen. They reckoned he suffocated doing nothing.

ELLIS? SAID BILLY.

What?

I said nice night for it, and he closed his locker.

Ellis picked up a coarse file and smashed it into a scrap panel.

There you go, Billy, he said. Knock it out.

IT WAS ONE in the morning. The canteen was busy and smelled of chips and shepherd's pie and something over-cooked and green. The sound of a radio crept out from the kitchen, Oasis, "Wonderwall," and the serving women sang along. Ellis was next in the queue. The light was harsh and he rubbed his eyes and Janice looked at him concerned. But then he said, Pie and chips, Janice, please.

And she said, Pie and chips it is then. There we go, my love. Gentlemen's portions, too.

Thanks.

Night, my love.

He walked over to the table in the far corner and pulled out a chair.

Do you mind, Glynn? he said.

Glynn looked up. Be my guest, he said. You all right there, Ellis mate?

Fine, he said, and he began to roll a cigarette. What's the book? he asked.

Harold Robbins. If I don't cover the front of it, you know what this lot are like. They'll make it smutty.

Any good?

Brilliant, said Glynn. Nothing predictable. The twists, the violence. Racy cars, racy women. Look. That's the photograph of the author. Look at him. Look at his *style*. That is my kind of man.

What's your kind of man? You a bit of a nelly, Glynn? said Billy, pulling up a chair.

In this context, my kind of man means the kind I'd hang out with.

Not us then?

I'd rather chew my hand off. No offense, Ellis.

None taken.

I was a bit like him in the seventies, style-wise, that is. You remember, Ellis?

A bit *Saturday Night Fever*, were you? said Billy.

I'm not listening to you.

White suit, gold chains?

Not listening.

All right, all right. Truce? said Billy.

Glynn reached across for the ketchup.

But, said Billy.

But what? said Glynn.

I bet you could tell by the way you used your walk that you were a woman's man with no time to talk.

What's he going on about? said Glynn.

No idea, said Ellis quietly, and he pushed his plate away.

OUT INTO THE NIGHT, he lit his cigarette. The temperature had dropped and he looked up and thought that snow was threatening. He said to Billy, You shouldn't wind Glynn up like that.

Billy said, He's asking for it.

No one's asking for it. And cut out the nelly shit.

Look, said Billy. Ursa Major. Can you see it? The Great Bear.

Did you hear me? said Ellis.

Look—down, down, down, up. Across. Down. And up, up. You see?

Did you hear me I said?

Yes, I heard you.

They walked back toward the Paint Shop. But did you see it? said Billy.

Oh Jesus, said Ellis.

THE HORN BLARED OUT and the assembly line slowed and the men busied themselves in handover and departure. It was seven in the morning and the morning was dark. Ellis wondered when he'd last seen the sun. He felt restless after shift, and when he felt like that he never went home straightaway because the loneliness would pounce. Sometimes, he cycled up to Shotover Woods, or out to Waterperry, just him filling the hours with the dull burn of miles in his calves. He'd watch the morning lighten against the trees and listen to birdsong to soothe his ears after the clash of industry. He tried not to think too much about things, out there in nature, and sometimes it worked and sometimes it didn't. When it didn't, he cycled back thinking his life was far from how he had intended it to be.

Along Cowley Road, orange streetlight scattered across the tar, and ghosts of shops long gone lurked in the mists of recollection. Betts, Lomas bike repair, Estelle's, Mabel's greengrocers, all gone. Had you told him as a boy that Mabel's wouldn't be here when he was a man, he never would have believed it. A junk shop called Second Time Around now stood in its place. It rarely opened.

He passed the old Regal Cinema, where thirty years ago Billy Graham, the evangelist preacher, had beamed out from the big screen to 1,500 of his faithful. Shopkeepers and passersby had gathered on the pavements to watch the masses stream out from its doors. Drinkers outside the City Arms pub had looked on awkwardly and shuffled their feet. It had been a standoff between excess and sobriety. But hadn't the road always been a point of tension between east and west? Two ends of the spectrum, the haves and have-nots, whether it be faith or money or tolerance.

He crossed Magdalen Bridge into the other country where the air smelled of books. He slowed to let a couple of students pass wearily in front of him—up early or still up late? It was hard to tell. He stopped and bought a cup of coffee and a newspaper down by the market. He cycled one-handed and drank it resting against a wall at the end of Brasenose Lane. He watched bleary-eyed tourists make use of a jet-lagged morning. Beautiful city you have here, one said. Yes, he said, and he drank his coffee.

. . .

THE FOLLOWING DAY, a Rover 600, pulled from the line, was waiting in the bay. Ellis checked the handover book and notes from the day shift. Another left front wing. He put on a pair of white cotton gloves from his pocket and spread out his fingers. He ran his fingertips across the damage line and could just feel the disparity, so slight that even light on paintwork could barely catch it. He stood upright and stretched out his back.

Billy. You try, he said.

Billy reached out. White gloves moving across the body. Pausing, retracing. Bingo.

There, said Billy.

You got it, said Ellis, and he picked up the dolly and spoon. Couple a taps, he said. That'll do it. Quick and light. There we go.

He checked the paintwork. It ran a perfect silver line, and Billy said, Did you always want to do this? And he surprised himself and said, No. And Billy said, What then? And he said, I wanted to draw.

The horn blared out and they walked out together into the biting freeze. Ellis pulled his hat down low and retied his scarf. His gloves came out of his pocket and he had to chase down a tissue that rolled away with a sudden gust of wind. He didn't mind Billy's laughter, Billy's laughter was easy.

I've got a date on Friday, said Billy.

Where you going?

Pub, I think. One in town. We're meeting by the Martyrs' Memorial.

Really? said Ellis. Where's your bike, by the way?

Over here near yours, said Billy. I don't know why I suggested meeting there, I couldn't think of anywhere else. And look at this, he said, pointing to the side of his nose. Spot.

You can hardly see it. You like this one?

Yeah, I like her, I really do. She's too good for me, said Billy.

And then Billy said, You have anyone, Ellis?

And he said, No.

And Billy said what no one else ever said. He said, Terry told me your wife died?

And the way he said it was gentle and direct and uninhibited, as if the death of love was normal.

She did, said Ellis.

How? said Billy.

Terry didn't tell you?

He told me to mind my own business. I can, you know. Mind it.

Car accident. Five years ago now.

Aw fuck, said Billy.

And Aw fuck was the only suitable answer, thought Ellis. Not, Oh sorry, or, That's awful. But Aw fuck. Billy was steering the conversation better than anyone had in a long time, and Billy said, Bet that's when you started on nights, right? I didn't think you did it for the money. I bet you couldn't sleep, right? I don't think I'd ever sleep again.

Billy and his nineteen years understood. They stopped at the gate and stood aside to let cars pass.

Billy said, I'm going to the Leys for a beer. Why don't you come?

I won't.

It's just me. And I like talking to you. You're not like the others.

The others are OK.

D'you ever go for a drink, Ell?

No.

Then I'm gonna keep trying. I'll make you my project.

Go on. Off you go.

See you tomorrow, Ell! and Ellis watched him disappear among the dozens of others heading out toward the estates of Blackbird Leys. He got on his bike and cycled slowly back west. He wondered when the kid had started calling him Ell.

It was eight in the morning and the sky across South Park had begun to lighten. Frost had settled on windscreens and birds' nests, and the pavements glistened. Ellis opened the front door and wheeled his bike into the hallway. The house felt cold and smelled of woodsmoke. In the back room he put his hand on the radiators. They were on, but they were battling. He didn't take his jacket off right away but stacked the hearth and got the flames going instead. He was good at building fires. He built the fires and Annie opened the wine, and the years rolled out. Thirteen, to be precise. Thirteen years of grapes and warmth.

He took a bottle of Scotch out of the cupboard and came back to the heat. In the silence, the echo of industry receded, just flames now, and the soft thud of car doors opening and shutting on a new day outside. This had always been the worst time, when the quiet emptiness could leave him gasping for breath. She was there, his wife, a peripheral shadow moving across a doorway, or in the reflection of a window, and he had to stop looking for her. And the whisky helped—helped him to walk past her when the fire was doused. But occasionally she followed him up the stairs and that's why he began to take the bottle with him, because she stood in the corner of their bedroom and watched him undress, and when he was on the verge of sleep, she leaned over him and asked him things like, Remember when we first met?

And he said, Of course I do. I was delivering a Christmas tree.

And?

And I rang your doorbell, smelling of pine and a bit of winter. And I saw your shadow approach through the window, and the door opened and there you were, plaid shirt and jeans and thick socks you wore as slippers. Your cheeks were bright, your eyes green, your hair splayed out across your shoulders, and in the lap of dusk it looked blonde, but later I would find hues of red. You were eating a crumpet, and the hallway smelled of crumpets, and you apologized and licked your fingers and I felt shy in my fur hat, so I pulled it off and held up the tree and said, This is yours, I presume, Miss Anne Cleaver? And you said, You presume right. Now take off your boots, and follow me. I kicked them off obediently, and followed and I never looked back.

I carried the tree into the front room where cloves had punctured the skin of oranges and I could see where you had been only minutes before. Your indent was still warm on the sofa with a book open to its side, a table with an empty plate, a cardigan, and the slow fade of a fire.

I placed the tree in its stand and helped you cover the

base with gold paper. From gold paper I moved to lights, from lights I moved to baubles, and from baubles, I reached up high and placed a star on top. When I came down I came down by your side, and didn't want to leave.

You said, Have you nowhere to go?

No, I said. Just back to the shop.

No trees to deliver?

No trees, I said. You were my last.

So what's at the shop? you said.

Michael. Mabel. And Scotch.

Ah, you said. That famous children's book!

I laughed.

You have a nice laugh, you said.

And then we didn't speak. Do you remember? Do you remember how you stared at me? How unnerved you made me feel? And I asked you why you were staring at me.

And you said, I'm wondering if I should take a chance on you.

And I said, Yes. Yes, is the only answer.

As dusk moved into darkness, we raced down South-field, holding hands, stopping once in the shadows where I tasted crumpets on your lips and tongue. We stopped at Cowley Road. The front display at Mabel's had been packed away and music blared out of the open door—"People Get Ready" by the Impressions. You squeezed my hand and told me it was a favorite of yours. Michael was alone in the shop, dancing and singing out loud to the song, and Sister Teresa was standing in the doorway watching him. We crossed the road and joined her. The music ended and we applauded and Michael took his bow. Sister said, Will you be coming to church this Christmas, Michael? We need singing like that.

He said, I'm afraid I won't, Sister. Church is not for me. And he said, Do you have everything you need for the big day? And she said, We do. And he said, Wait, and went into the back. Here, he said.

Mistletoe, she laughed. Long time since I stood beneath that, and she wished us all a Merry Christmas and left.

And who is this? said Michael, turning his gaze on you. I said, This is Anne. And you said, Annie, actually. And he said, Ms. Annie Actually. I like her.

The year was 1976. You were thirty. Me, twenty-five.

These are the details you never thought I'd remember.

We all three sat outside in the garden behind the shop. It was cold but I didn't feel cold with you by my side. Mabel came out to say hello, and you stood up, said, Sit here, Mabel. And she said, Not tonight. I'm going to bed to listen to the music. What music? you said. But she didn't hear, just disappeared back inside.

We built a fire in the middle of bricks and we drank

beer and ate baked potatoes and sank down into blankets as our breath misted, as stars appeared as fragile as ice crystals. The sound of a trumpet interrupted our words and we all three jumped at the back wall and held ourselves up by our fingers, as we looked across the wild and overgrown churchyard. We saw the dark silhouette of a trumpet player leaning against a tree.

Who's that? you asked.

Dexter Shawlands, said Michael.

Who's he? you said.

An old flame of Mabel's. Comes here once a year to play her song.

That's love, you said.

THE NEXT DAY, the alarm went off at five in the afternoon as it always did. Ellis sat up sharply. His throat felt tight and his heart was racing. Whatever confidence he had in himself had disappeared in his sleep. He knew this mood and it was a fucker of a mood because it was unpredictable, and he rolled out of bed before he couldn't. He turned off the alarm and it would be his first triumph of the day. The second would be cleaning his teeth. The room felt cold and he went to the window. Streetlights and gloom. The phone rang and he let it ring.

The first flurry of snow fell as he cycled down Divinity Road. There was a weight to his body, and he'd tried to explain it once, to a doctor, but he never really had the words. It was a feeling, that's all, an overwhelming feeling that started in his chest and made his eyelids heavy. A shutting down that weakened his hands and made it hard to breathe. When he passed through the gates of the factory he couldn't remember the journey at all.

He spent the hours preoccupied and distant, and those who knew his history warned others with a quick nod or wink in his direction, meaning "wide berth, fellas," and even Billy kept his head down. During a lull, he sat against his locker and took out his tobacco and began to roll. Billy stopped him and said, What you doing, Ell? And Ellis stared at him and felt the kid's hand on his shoulder. Bell's gone, said Billy. Dinner, Ellis. Come on. Let's get your stuff.

In the canteen, he could feel his leg twitch. His mouth was dry and there was too much noise, it was all around him and under his skin, he could feel his heart thumping.

And the smell of cooking was overwhelming and he had a plate piled high with food because word had gone round and Janice felt sorry for him, so she piled the plate high, and men nearby complained, but she shut them up with that certain look she had. And now Billy and Glynn were at it. Ever read *The Stud*, Glynn? Who hasn't? Should be on the national curriculum. Ever done it on a swing, Glynn? I have actually, you ignorant twat. Oh yeah? Children's playground?

The noise. The fucking noise, and he got up from the table. And he was outside and snow was falling and he could hear it fall. Look up, look up and he did. He opened his mouth and caught snow on his tongue. And he was calm again, out there alone, just him and snow. The noise settled and the quiet drone of traffic lifted into the sky.

Billy came out and saw him looking up with tears frozen before they could fall. And he wanted to say to Billy, I'm just trying to hold it all together, that's all.

He wanted to say that because he'd never been able to say that to anyone, and Billy might be a good person to say it to. But he couldn't. So he walked past him without look- ing, walked past and ignored him just as his father would have done.

He didn't go back to the line. He got on his bike and began to ride. The back wheel pulled away every now and then, but the main roads had been salted, and soon he was racing away, thinking about nothing, a body expending so much effort trying to escape from something he could never put words to. When he got to Cowley Road he was distracted by a light coming out of Mabel's old shop, and that's why he didn't see the car until it was too late. It sped out of Southfield and it happened so quick, the terror of freefall. He stretched out his arm to lessen the impact and when the curb rushed up at him he heard the crack in his wrist, and the heavy thud winded him. He saw the tail-lights of a car moving away, heard the rhythmic sound of rotating bike wheels. He let his head rest against the cold pavement and the weight lifted. He could breathe again.

A man ran out of the dark and said, I've called an ambulance. And the man crouched down at his side and said, Are you all right?

Never better, said Ellis.

Don't sit up, said the man.

But he did sit up and he looked about at the snow. What's your name? asked the man. Where d'you live? The sound of a siren coming toward them, getting louder. And Ellis thinking, All this fuss over nothing. I've never felt so clear.

WHEN HE WAS SMALL, Ellis remembered how he used to like to watch his father shave. He used to sit on the toilet cistern with his feet dangling, looking up at his father because his father was so big. The air was steamy and the mirror dripped with condensation and neither said a word. His father wore a vest, and sunlight streamed through the window and fell on his shoulders and chest, and his skin was patterned by fleurs-de-lis that had been carved into the glass, and the overall effect made his father look as if he had been sculpted from the finest marble.

He remembered how he watched his father pull his skin this way and that way, drawing the razor across the bristles, the sound of sandpaper in the folds of soap. And sometimes he would whistle a tune of the time, and then *tap tap tap*, the foam fell into the steaming water and small black flecks settled against the white porcelain and remained there, a tidemark, when the basin ran dry. And he remembered thinking that his father could do anything and was afraid of nothing. And those large hands that liked to spar in the boxing ring were also capable of beautiful gestures, like splashing onto his cheeks and neck the sweet musky scent that completed him.

And once, in that sweet state of completeness, Ellis reached out and held him. A brief moment of ownership before his father's grip tore into his arms and wrenched them away, before the sound of a door slam instantly replaced the *tap tap tap* of love. And Ellis remembered thinking how he would have given anything to have been like his father, anything. Before the pain of that memory stopped him reaching for him again.

He didn't know why he thought of this now, lying in his

bed, plastered from hand to elbow, and he could only conclude it was because earlier in the hospital, the nurse had asked him if there was anyone she could contact.

No, he'd said. My father's away on holiday in Bournemouth with his woman, Carol. She wears strong perfume. That's how I know when she's been around. They always thought I never knew but I did. The perfume, see?

Talking bollocks because of the drugs.

And now he was in his own bed, staring at the ceiling, thinking of all the things he could have done that would have made this moment more convenient. Top of the list, he thought, was a Teasmade. They were ugly. But they were useful. He just wanted a cup of tea. Or coffee. Something warm and sweet, but maybe that was simply the shock coming out. He felt so cold, pulled on a T-shirt he found under his pillow. He thought the room was shabby. All the jobs he never finished. All the jobs he'd never *started*. A garage full of oak floorboards, five years in the waiting.

Music from next door bled into the room. Marvin Gaye, old-school seduction. It was the students. He didn't mind them, they were company of sorts, and he sat up and reached for a glass of water. He used to be friends with his neighbors but he wasn't so good at it now. He used to be in and out of their homes, but that was before. But his neigh-

bors were now students and, next year, there would be another bunch not to get to know. He looked at his watch. He
leaned across the bedside table and took out a Voltarol and
co-codamol and finished the last of his water. He exercised
his fingers as best he could but they felt stiff and swollen.
He wasn't sure what the bottle of whisky was doing next to
his bed. It was that fairy again, he thought.

The music from next door turned to sex, and he was
surprised because he'd assumed sex was not a frequent oc-
currence for the students next door. They studied statistics
and, statistically, they had little chance against the kids
studying literature or philosophy. Or art, come to that.
Well, that's what he thought. It was just the way it was,
some subjects were sexy. The bed was knocking against
the wall, they were hard at it. He lay back down and started
to drift off to the sound of a young woman coming.

When he woke again, the clock said seven. It was dark
outside and streetlights lit his room. It could be morning,
though it was probably evening. Absolute silence in the
world. Nobody watching out for him. He rolled out of bed
and stood up shakily. He felt bruised and tender and could
see mauve shadowing spreading across his thigh. He went
across to the bathroom.

When he came back he poured out a small measure of
Scotch in his water glass. He stood at the window and drew

the curtains wide. South Park was dusted in white and the streets were empty. He drank the whisky and leaned against the books. He glanced down at the photo of the three of them, Michael, him and Annie. Annie loved her books. That's how he'd surprised her on their sixth wedding anniversary. Led her blindfolded from her job at the library, to what would become her own bookshop in St. Clements, and there, restored her sight with two brass keys. Michael had been waiting inside with champagne, of course. What am I going to call this place? she said, as the cork flew across the floor. Annie and Co., they suggested, trying hard not to sound too practiced.

Ellis flicked the catches and opened the window wide. He shuddered, unprepared for the incoming freeze. He knelt down and stuck his arm out the window. He clenched his fingers, opened his fingers. Clenched them, opened them. He was diligent and did exactly what the nurse had told him to do. He suddenly felt tired again and the bed looked far away. He tugged at the duvet and pulled it toward him. He wrapped himself up and fell asleep on the floor.

The heat of the room eventually woke him. He was wedged up against the radiator after a restless night of bad thinking. He had no idea what day it was but had a sudden recollection of a phone call with Carol, a promise to check the heating in their house later that day. He sat up and smelled his armpits. There was something murky lurking in the fibers, and he got up and went across to the bathroom and ran a bath. The throbbing in his hand had subsided and he wrapped his arm in a plastic bag as the nurse had told him to.

OUT IN THE GARDEN, the crisp air felt good to breathe. Blue skies had nudged out the gray of yesterday and for a brief moment, in the faint rays of winter sunshine, the promise of a new season teased and the snow had already turned to mush in its presence. Ellis leaned back against the kitchen wall with the sun on his face.

You all right, Ellis?

Ellis opened his eyes. He was surprised the young man standing at the fence knew his name.

Yeah, not too bad, he said.

What happened?

Ellis smiled. Fell off my bike, he said.

Shit, said the student.

Wait, said the student, and he disappeared inside. He came back out with a steaming mug.

There you go, he said. Coffee. And he lifted the mug across the fence.

And Ellis didn't know what to say. He felt fucked up a bit from the pills and the sleep but it wasn't that really, it was the gesture that unsettled him, the kindness that made the words catch in his throat and, eventually, he said, Thank you. Thank you, your name, I—

Jamie.

Yes, right. Jamie. Of course. Sorry.

Anyway, enjoy it. I'm going back in. If you need anything, let us know.

And the kid was gone. Ellis sat down on the bench.

The coffee was good, it wasn't instant, it was real and strong, and stopped the hunger. He needed to shop. He couldn't remember when he ate more than toast. He drank the coffee and looked across the garden. It had been quite a haven once. Annie'd had the vision and she'd turned it into a seasonal palette of rotating color. She took out books and studied them late into the night, sketched out her ideas. She halved the lawn and planted flowers and shrubs he could never pronounce. Tall grasses became water in the wind, and around the bench the joy of nasturtiums every summer. You can't kill nasturtiums, she'd once declared, but he had. All those delicate, brilliant ideas had withered in the shade of his neglect. Only the hardy remained beneath the overgrown brambles. Honeysuckle trailers, camellias, they were all in there somewhere, and he could see thick clusters of scarlet heads shining out of the undergrowth like lanterns. Weeds grew around him, along the borders by the back door and kitchen. He bent down and picked up a handful and they came away surprisingly easily from the soil.

He felt warm liquid trickle from his nose and he wondered if he had the start of a cold. He searched for a handkerchief but had to make do with the hem of his shirt. When he looked down he saw blood. He held his hand under his chin and caught the pooling blood as best he could. He went back into the kitchen and pulled off a wad of kitchen roll, which he clamped hard to his nose.

He sat down on the cold tiled floor and leaned back against the fridge. As he reached for more paper, it was then that he imagined his wife's hand instead. He closed his eyes. Felt her hand in his hand and the softness of her lips leaving a shimmering trail across his arm.

You're so distant these days, she said.

I'm an idiot.

You are, she said, and laughed. What's got into you?

I'm stuck.

Still? she said.

All the things you were going to do, she said.

I miss you.

Come on, she said. You could still do them. This isn't about me. You know that, right, Ellis?

Ell?

Where have you gone?

I'm here, he said.

You keep fading out. You're really annoying these days.

Sorry.

I said, This isn't about me.

I know.

Go find him, she said.

Annie?

He kept his eyes closed long after she was gone. He felt the cold of the room, the hard floor. He heard blackbirds and the persistent drone of a fridge. He opened his eyes and pulled the compress away from his nose. Not bleeding now. He staggered up and felt so much space around him he almost choked.

BY THE AFTERNOON the snow had virtually gone but he kept to the roads because the roads had been salted. At Cowley Road he waited for a break in the traffic and crossed. He looked about for his bike but couldn't see it in the vicinity. He couldn't imagine anyone would want it, top of the range it wasn't. Cost him fifty quid ten years ago and even then, everyone said he'd been done. Time for a change, he thought. The pain in his arm prompting his sudden equanimity.

He remembered the night of his accident, how he had been distracted by a light in Mabel's old shop, and he turned back toward it and tried the door. It was locked, of course, with no sign that anyone had been about. He peered through the opaque swirls of dried Windex into a ramshackle interior overflowing with junk. He found it hard to equate that cluttered space with the one of his boyhood. A faded green curtain used to hang at the back, separating commerce from home. To the right of the curtain, a table. On top of the table a cash register, a record player and two piles of records. The display at the front was made up of sacks of vegetables and crates of fruit. In the middle, opposite the door, an armchair that smelled of tangerines every time you sat in it. How was it possible the three of them had moved about this space with unequivocal ease?

It was Mabel who had asked him to join her the night Michael arrived in Oxford after his father's death. A friendly face of similar age to her grandson. He remembered standing where he was standing now. Him and Mabel, the welcome party. Both nervous, both quiet. The streets silenced by snow.

For years after, Mabel used to say that Michael came with the snow because that was the only way she could remember the year he moved in with her. January '63, it was, thought Ellis. We were twelve. Thereabouts.

They watched Mr. Khan's minicab slow down and stop in front of the shop. He got out of his car and raised his hands skyward, and said, Oh, Mrs. Wright! What a wonderful thing is snow!

And Mabel said, You'll catch your death out here, Mr. Khan. You're not used to it. Now did you remember my grandson?

Oh, indeed! he said, and he raced round to the passenger door and opened it.

One prodigal grandson, he said, with two suitcases full of books.

Come in, come in, said Mabel, and the three of them huddled around a small electric heater that was losing the fight against the night's sudden freeze. Mr. Khan walked through with the suitcases and disappeared into the back, his footsteps heavy on the stairs and on the landings overhead. Mabel introduced the boys and they shook hands formally and said hello, before self-consciousness stifled them. Ellis noticed the cowlick at the front of Michael's cropped dark hair and the horizontal scar above his upper lip—the result of a fall against a table, he'd later learn—a feature that, in the wrong sort of light, could turn his smile into an unexpected sneer: an idiosyncrasy that would become more developed over the years.

Ellis went to the window. The clock ticked quietly behind him, light from the Italian café spilled yellow onto the white street in front. He heard Mabel say, I expect you're hungry, and Michael said, No, not really, and he came and stood next to Ellis, instead. They looked at one another in the reflection of the glass and snow fell behind their eyes. They watched a nun make slow and careful progress toward the church of St. Mary and St. John next door. Mr. Khan came back into the room and pointed.

Look! he said. Penguin! he said, and they laughed.

Later that night, in Michael's room, Ellis said, Are they really full of books?

No, just the one, said Michael as he opened a suitcase.

I don't read, said Ellis.

What's that then? said Michael, pointing to the black book in Ellis's hand.

My sketchbook. I take it everywhere.

Can I see?

Sure, and Ellis handed over his book.

Michael flicked through the pages, acknowledging images with a slow nod of his head. He suddenly stopped. Who's that? he said, holding open a page at a woman's face.

My mother.

Does she really look like that? asked Michael.

Yes.

She's beautiful.

Is she?

Don't you think so?

She's my *mother*.

Mine left.

Why?

He shrugged. Just walked out.

D'you think she'll come back?

I'm not sure she knows where I am anymore, and he handed back the sketchbook. You can draw me if you want, he said.

OK, said Ellis. Now?

No. In a couple of days, he said. Make me look interesting. Make me look like a poet.

ELLIS TURNED AWAY from the window. A bus inched into view and he crossed the road and waved it down. He sat alone at the back and closed his eyes. He felt groggy all of a sudden. The disorientation of mixing memory and medication.

. . .

HE RARELY WENT to his father's house when nobody was there, rarely went when only his father was there, truth be told. He did anything to avoid the wordless connection neither felt comfortable with. He got off the bus before he needed to and walked the rest of the way under a sky that was becoming overcast again. What was it about these roads that plunged him into a state of childlike anxiety?

The light had virtually disappeared by the time he reached the front door, and a feeling of foreboding had taken hold. He put the key in the lock. Inside, the sound of traffic retreated and the gray light darkened, and it could have been evening. He felt nervous and unsure, now it was just him alone with the years.

The house was warm, and that was all Carol had wanted to know, whether they'd left the heating on to counteract the imminent freeze. He could go now, and yet he didn't. The perverse pull of the past drew him inside to the back room, virtually unaltered since the days of his youth.

The room smelled of dinner, still. A roast. They always had a roast the night before they went away because they never knew what the food would be like at the hotel. That was his father's thinking for sure. He looked about.

The table, the dresser—that dark slab of oppressive oak— the mirror, so little had changed. The armchairs might have been re-covered but tug away the maroon and navy fabric and the melancholic imprint of the past was still there. He opened the curtains and looked out onto the gar- den. Faint patches of snow amidst the rockery.

Crocus heads wistful and purple, and the car factory over there showing a fake dusk. He noticed the carpet had been changed but the overwhelming hue of brown hadn't. Maybe Carol had put her foot down? Maybe she had said either it goes or I go. Maybe Carol was the kind of woman who could make those demands without repercussion. He stood in front of the wall opposite the door where his mother's painting of the *Sunflowers* used to hang.

She would suddenly stop in front of that painting, and whatever she was saying or doing at that precise moment came to an abrupt halt in the presence of the color yellow. It was her solace. Her inspiration and confessional.

One afternoon, not long after Michael had come to live in Oxford, they came back to the house together and it was the first time his mother, Dora, and Michael had met. He remembered how charmed they were by one another, how engaged they were in conversation almost immediately, how Michael maneuvered her seamlessly into the space his own mother had vacated.

He remembered how Michael stood in front of the painting of the *Sunflowers* with his mouth wide open and said, Is that an original, Mrs. Judd?

And his mother said, No! Good Lord no—how I wish it was! No. I won it in a raffle.

I was just going to say that had it been an original, then it might be of considerable value.

His mother stared at him and said, How funny you are.

She brought sandwiches in from the kitchen and placed the plate down in front of them and said, D'you know who painted it?

Van Gogh, said Michael.

Dora looked at her son and laughed. You told him.

I didn't! he protested.

He didn't, said Michael. I know quite a lot.

Eat, she said, and the boys reached for the plate.

He cut his ear off, said Michael.

That's right, said Dora.

With a razor, said Michael.

Why'd he do that? asked Ellis.

Who knows? said his mother.

Madness, said Michael.

You don't say? said Ellis.

I would've cut off something more discreet, said Michael. Like a toe.

All right, all right, said Dora. Enough now. D'you know where van Gogh came from, Michael?

Yes. Holland. Same as Vermeer.

See—he really does know a lot, said Ellis.

You're right, said Dora. Holland. And the colors he was familiar with there were earth colors, dark colors, you know, browns and grays. Dark greens. And the light was like here, flat and uninspiring. And he wrote to his brother Theo that he had a great desire to go south—to Provence in France, that is—to search for something different, a different way of painting. To become a better artist.

I like to imagine how it would have been for him, stepping out of the train station at Arles into such an intense yellow light. It changed him. How could it not? How could it not change anyone?

Would you like to go south, Mrs. Judd? asked Michael.

And his mother laughed and said, I'd like to go anywhere!

Where's Arles? said Ellis.

Shall we see, said his mother, and she went to the dresser and pulled out an atlas.

The pages fell open heavily at North America, and a cloud of dust rose. Ellis leaned forward as countries and continents and oceans flicked by. His mother slowed at Europe, stopped at France.

Here we are, she said. Near Avignon. Saint-Rémy and Arles. That's where he painted. He searched for light and sun, and found both. And he did what he set out to do. Painted using primary colors, and their complements, too.

What's a complement? Ellis asked.

Complementing colors are ones that make the other stand out. Like blue and orange, said his mother, as if reciting off the page.

Like me and Ellis, said Michael.

Yes, she smiled. Like you two. And primary colors are?

Yellow, blue and red, said Ellis.

That's it, said Dora.

And the composites are orange, green and purple, said Michael.

Bingo! said Dora. So who wants cake?

We haven't got to the *Sunflowers* yet, said Michael.

No, we haven't, she said. You're right. OK, so Vincent hoped to set up an artists' studio down there in the South because he was keen to have friends and like-minded people around him.

I think he was probably lonely, said Michael. What with the ear thing and the darkness.

I think he was, too, said Dora. 1888 was the year, and he was waiting for another artist to join him, a man called Paul Gauguin. People say that, in all probability, he painted the *Sunflowers* as decoration for Gauguin's room. Did lots of versions of them too, not just this. It's a lovely thought, though, isn't it? Some people say it's not true but I like to think it is. Painting flowers as a sign of friendship and welcome. Men and boys should be capable of beautiful things. Never forget that, you two, she said, and she disappeared into the kitchen.

They listened to the sound of a cake being brought to a plate, a cutlery drawer opened, Dora's happiness in a song.

And look how he painted! said Dora, suddenly propelled back into the room by a new thought. Look at the brushstrokes, you can see them. Thick and robust. Whoever copied this, copied his style too because he liked to paint fast, as if he was in the grip of something. And when it all comes together—the light, the color, the passion, it's—

The sound of a key in the lock made her fall silent. His father strode past them into the kitchen. He said nothing but made noise. Kettle heavy on the stove, cups, drawers opening, banging shut.

I'm out tonight, said his father.

Fine, said Dora, and she watched him leave the room with a mug of tea.

And when it all comes together? asked Ellis.

It's *life*, said his mother.

THE FOLLOWING SUNDAY, snow had fallen hard and had settled well, and his mother drove them out to Brill with the toboggan. It was the first of many memories he had, of how Michael sought Dora's attention in those early days, how he clung to her every word as if they were handholds up a cliff face. He said he had to sit in the front on account of car sickness, and he spent the entire journey complimenting Dora on her driving and her style, steering the conversation back to the *Sunflowers* and the South, back to color and light. Had he been able to change gears for her, Ellis firmly believed he would have.

His mother got out of the car and buttoned up her coat. She said, Don't forget to look around you when you get to the top. Take it all in as if you were going to paint it. You may never see snow like this again. See how it changes the landscape. See how it changes you.

I will, said Michael, and he marched on ahead, full of purpose. Ellis looked at his mother and smiled.

They dragged the toboggan through snowdrifts and up steep edges and flowing inclines to the windmill, and to the view of the ermine hills and farmland around. And they could see Dora in the distance. Wrapped in a red coat and thick scarf, she was leaning against the engine, warming herself, a plume of smoke curling from the corner of her red lips. Michael raised his arm. I don't think she can see me, he said. She can see you, said Ellis, positioning the toboggan at the edge of the slope. Michael waved again. Eventually, Dora waved back. Come on, let's go, said Ellis. One last look around, said Michael.

Ellis sat at the front and gripped the rope hard, his feet resting on the runners. He felt Michael clamber on behind him. Felt his hands reach around his waist. Ready? he said. Ready, Michael said. And they nudged the toboggan forward until it pulled away over the side, and they were thrown back by gathering speed and unexpected troughs, hidden beneath the drifts. He could feel Michael tight around his waist, his scream in his ear, as they bounced down the hill, trees an indecipherable blur, racing past those coming up, and then all of a sudden, there was no traction, there was only air and flight, and them, and they were peeled away from one another, and from rope and wood, and they fell to earth, winded and dazed, tumbling in a flurry of snow and sky and laughter, and they only slowed when the land flattened out, when it brought them back together again and held them still.

· · ·

SHORTLY AFTER HIS fourteenth birthday, Ellis came
home from school and saw his mother sitting quietly in
front of her painting. The scene reminded him of being in
church, watching the kneeling in front of devotional pan-
els, prayers hoping to be heard. He didn't disturb her, he
remembered, because her demeanor and intensity frightened him. He went upstairs to his room and put the image
behind him as best he could.

In the days that followed, however, he couldn't help but
watch her. Shopping trips had her pausing for breath along
streets she used to race down. Dinners once devoured with
delight were picked at, refrigerated, later binned. And one
Saturday when his father was at the boxing club and he was
doing his homework upstairs, he heard the crash of plates
and ran down to the kitchen. His mother was still on the
floor when he got to her, and before he could brush up the
broken china, she reached for his hand and said something
strange, said, You'll stay on at school till you're eighteen,
won't you? And you'll do your art? Ellis? Look at me.
You'll—

—Yes, he said. Yes.

That night in his room, he searched for signs of something wrong in his sketchbooks old and new. The draw-

ings he'd made of his mother a year ago compared to the ones of now were proof on the page because he knew her face so well. Her eyes were sunken and the light they emitted was dusk not dawn. She was thinner too, sharp around her temples, her nose more pronounced. Really, though, it was about her touch and gaze, because when either fell on him, neither wanted to let him go.

The next day, he got up early and went straight to Mabel's. She was cleaning the front window and was surprised to see him so early and she said, Michael's still in his room, and he said, I think Mum's ill. She stopped what she was doing and drove him back home. Dora opened the door and Mabel said, He knows.

His father went on nights, which surprised no one. He escaped his wife's nighttime fears and left her in the care of her son. Mabel instructed him in basic cooking and housekeeping, and she concocted a menu for him that included leftovers and an ever-changing stew. After school, Michael came back with him and they built fires for Dora and kept her warm and entertained with stories.

Michael said, Listen to this, Dora—Mrs. Copsey stormed into the shop yesterday and said (and he imitated her), What in God's name is that next to the cauliflower, Mrs. Wright? It's okra, said Mabel. Mrs. Khan asked me to get some. But they have their own shops down past the Co-op, said Mrs. Copsey. But Mrs. Khan likes to shop with me, said Mabel. That may be so, said Mrs. Copsey. But put out rubbish, Mrs. Wright, and you'll attract flies.

She didn't! said his mother.

She *did*, said Michael. And then she said—These people just don't know how to be English, Mrs. Wright. But they're not English, said Mabel, and you said the same about the Welsh twenty years ago. Good day to you, Mrs. Copsey. Careful of the flies!

And Michael reached for Dora's hand and they laughed and Ellis remembered how grateful he was that Michael's care was instinctive and natural because he could never be that way with her. He was constantly on the lookout for the last good-bye.

Her illness advanced rapidly, and between pillows of morphine, brief moments of consciousness would arise where the two of them would always be waiting for her with an idea—

I was thinking about color and light, said Michael. And I was thinking maybe that's all we are, Dora. Color and light.

Or with a distraction—

Look, Dora. Ellis has drawn me, and Michael held up the sketchbook. Dora reached over and held her son's hand

and told him how clever he was to draw so well. Never stop, will you? she said. Promise me.

I promise.

Make him promise, Michael.

I will, Dora.

Two months after Ellis had first suspected something, his mother went into hospital. As she left the house, she said, I'll see you later, Ell. Don't forget to wash and don't forget to eat.

It was the last time he saw her.

The emptiness of the house overwhelmed him and he couldn't free himself from the sudden panic that ambushed him when the curtains were drawn. Some days he smelled perfume, too, that wasn't his mother's and it made him sick. In the end, he packed a bag and went to stay at Mabel's. He was never sure if his father had noticed he was gone.

Working in the shop at weekends was a good distraction, and brought back his appetite for food. But it was the routine of being cared for again that was the silent wonder. He stood taller. That's what people noticed.

He and Michael were in the shop the day Mabel returned from the ward and told them Dora had died. Michael ran up to his room, and Ellis wanted to follow him but his legs wouldn't move, a sudden moment of paralysis that marked the end of childhood.

Ellis? said Mabel.

He couldn't speak, he couldn't cry. Staring at the floor, struggling to remember the color of his mother's eyes, just something to hold on to, but he couldn't. Only later would Michael tell him they were green.

Funeral day, and they stood in silence at the dining table making sandwiches. He buttered, Mabel filled, Michael cut. The only sound in the room came from his father, who was polishing his leather work boots. The angry scratch of bristles being worked across the toe. The sound of spit, sharp and incessant against a clock counting down. A hearse pulling up outside.

In Rose Hill chapel, Ellis sat at the front next to his father. The organ sounded much too loud and his mother's coffin looked much too small. He smelled the same perfume he noticed on occasion at home, and when he turned round, sitting behind him was a woman with peroxide-blonde hair and a kind smile, and she leaned forward and whispered, Don't forget, Ellis, your dad needs you: a declaration as shocking to him as his mother's death. He stood up, an action so instinctive it caught him by surprise. And years later, he came to believe that the courage it took for him to walk out of church that afternoon, amidst the whispers and stares, used up his life's quota.

He hitched a ride down to the river and the man in the

car said, Cheer up, mate! You look like you've been to a funeral. And Ellis said he had, said it was his mum's, and the man said Christ, and said nothing after that. Took him to the gates at Iffley Lock and handed him a fiver when he got out. Ellis asked what the money was for and the man said he didn't know. Just take it, he said.

He crossed the lock and walked the towpath to Long Bridges bathing place, his and Michael's favorite hangout. The trees had passed through autumn and it should have been cold but an unseasonal warm breeze followed him under Donnington Bridge, gathering up geese, launching them into flight.

At the bathing place he found himself alone. He sat down next to the steps. The call of ducks, the sound of a train, oars slapping against the water: life in continuum. He wondered when the sun would shine hot again, and an hour later, Michael shouted to him from the bridge and ran toward him. When Michael was near, Ellis said, What are we going to do without her?

And Michael said, We carry on and we don't give up. And he knelt down and kissed him. It was their first kiss. Something good in a day of bad.

They sat there quietly, not talking about death, or the kiss, or how life was going to change. They watched the shifting colors of the sun and the deep shadows eavesdropped on their grief, and the vivid descant of birdsong slowly muted to unimaginable silence.

He never knew what made him look up, but when he did his father was watching them from the bridge. He didn't know how long he had been there but a knot of tension bedded down in his gut. He knew his father hadn't seen them kiss but the proximity of their bodies couldn't be mistaken. Knee against knee, arm against arm, the clasp of hands out of sight, or so he thought. His father stayed where he was and shouted, Come on, let's go! And when they got to him, he didn't look at them but turned and started walking away.

His father drove badly, slipping gears, braking sharply, a wonder he never killed anyone. He dropped Michael at the shop and when Ellis was about to get out too, his father said, Not tonight, you're not. You stay here.

The car journey home was oppressive and made in silence. The pain in his stomach grew and he felt so adrift in the care of this man. This man who didn't really know him, this man who had just stalled in the middle of a junction, who was slumped over the steering wheel as horns blared, who kept saying, Fuck fuck, over and over. Ellis opened the car door and walked away.

He walked aimlessly till night fell. He bought chips and ate them on the street, sitting with his back against a wall, his mum would have been so ashamed. He only returned home when he was convinced his father would have passed out on a bed or floor upstairs.

The lights were out when he entered the hallway. Quietly, he placed his foot on the first stair when a voice startled him and drew him back into the darkness of the front room.

In here, said his father, switching on the standard lamp at his side. He stood up from the sofa and the plastic sheeting crackled with static. In his hand, one of Ellis's sketchbooks.

You're getting soft, he said, flicking through the pages. Look how soft you've got, and he threw the book across the floor. It opened at a drawing of Michael.

He said, Let me tell you something. What you *want* to do and what you're *going* to do are two very different things. You're leaving school year after next.

I'm not, said Ellis.

I've got you an apprenticeship at the Car Plant.

Mum said—

—She's not here.

Let me stay till I'm eighteen. Please.

Get into guard.

Eighteen. I'll do anything after that.

Get. Into. Guard. The. Way. I. Taught. You.

Ellis raised his fists reluctantly. He watched his father pick up his work boots and put one on each hand, the hard leather soles facing out toward him.

Right now, said his father. Punch.

What?

Punch my hands.

No.

Fucking punch them. Punch them.

I said punch them.

And Ellis punched.

HE COULD BARELY hold the phone, let alone dial. But thirty minutes later, Mabel stood at the door, her night-dress glimpsed below her coat. He remembered how she walked into the house and told Leonard Judd to stay away from her and not to speak till she was good and ready. She went upstairs with Ellis and put a few of his clothes and schoolbooks into a bag. She led him out to the van and drove back to the shop.

When she stopped at the lights she said, Bide your time, Ellis.

Mum wanted me to do my art, he said.

You don't need a canvas to do that, she said. I knew a tinny, once, who worked on those cars as if he'd sculpted them himself. Make peace with it, my boy. Make your peace.

They pulled up outside the shop. Faint light from the kitchen edged through the curtain at the back. Mabel said, While I'm here, you always have a home. You know that? This is your key. I'll leave it on the hook in the kitchen. And when you're ready, you take it.

Thank you, Mabel.

The clock in the kitchen said two seventeen. Mabel opened the fridge and wrapped the contents of an ice tray in a cloth. Hold this against your hands, she said, and Ellis took the wrap and followed her up the stairs.

He said good night outside her room and continued up to the top bedroom. He opened the door and the room was dark and smelled of Michael. He could see the dark shape of his body sitting up in bed. He went over and lay next to him.

He's making me leave school, he said. I'm going to the factory. Just like he did. Just like they did bef—

—Shh, said Michael, and he took the ice and held it against his hand. He'll change his mind, he said. We'll make him. Mabel will.

You think? said Ellis.

I think, said Michael.

And when the house fell silent they shared a bed. They

kissed, took off their tops. And Ellis couldn't believe a body could feel so good when an hour before he was in despair.

Three months, it took, before he felt able to go back to his father's, and when he did, circumstances had changed. The peroxide blonde had moved in, and her perfume was familiar and strong, and she had a name and her name was Carol. She sat in his mum's chair and the painting was off the wall. Welcome back, son, his father said.

THE INTRUSIVE TICK of the clock brought Ellis back to the present. He stared at the blank wall. Pieces of a jig-saw, that's all the past was now. He left a note propped up on the table hoping his dad and Carol had a good holiday. *P.S.*, he wrote. *Any idea where Mum's painting might have gone?*

He closed the front door and a mizzle of rain met his face. Streetlights hovered in the damp gloom and he won-dered, briefly, when the clocks were going forward. He knew his mood would lighten with the sky.

ELLIS LEFT the fracture clinic with his arm replastered and another six weeks off work. The freedom this afforded him lifted his spirit and gave him a purpose that had long eluded him. He decided not to go home right away, but to continue into Headington to do a much-needed shop. He bought steak and fish and vegetables, ingredients he would try to use imaginatively, and he bought a bottle of wine (screwcap), and bread (sliced) from the baker. The flowers were an afterthought, the strong espresso, too, bought from the new café across the road. He got it to take away with a piece of banana bread that was still warm.

The day stayed dull, but there was no threat of rain, so he continued to journey on foot, and by the time he reached the gates of Holy Trinity, the shopping bag felt heavy and the bruise around his leg made him slow. He sat on the bench and looked out over the churchyard. He had imagined the graves would look bleak, suffering the aftermath of snow, but it was March and already the daffodils were standing proud. He could see Annie's grave over to the left, but he drank his coffee first and ate the cake, which had a surprising touch of cinnamon.

The churchyard had been one of Annie's favorite places to go and read. It was out of the way, but summer days she got on her bike and she made the effort. The air hazy with pollen, the sound of organ practice behind her, the occasional call of a pheasant in the field beyond. That was the reason they'd chosen to get married there.

A wedding, more real than perfect. That's how Michael

liked to describe it, and he was right. Annie's dress was unconventional. Knee-length, white cotton with navy embroidery, vintage French. Michael had taken her to London to buy it. He'd helped her with the makeup too. Colors that highlighted happiness over cheekbones. Annie had wanted him to walk her down the aisle but Ellis had already nabbed him for best man. I could do both, he said, enthusiastically. The wedding, so suddenly, all about him.

In the end, Mabel performed the duty, a sweet twist on convention. You be good to her, she whispered to Ellis, as she handed the bride ceremoniously to him.

As husband and wife, they came back down the aisle to Maria Callas singing "*O mio babbino caro*," a much talked-about choice. Her voice followed them out of the church into intermittent sunshine and a small gathering of friends and family. It was beautiful, it was theater. It was Michael and Annie's idea. Everything memorable came from them, he thought. In the stillness of air, confetti landed where it was thrown, and in the photographs that were to follow, heads and shoulders would be dusted in pink.

He finished his coffee and watched a group of American tourists look for C. S. Lewis's grave. They'll see the sign in a moment, he thought. He stood up, picked up his bag and veered through the graves to the spectacle of color the other side of the tree.

The daffodils were a mix of white and yellow, and he knew they were his father's doing. A groundcover of forget-me-nots, too, not yet in bloom, the man was so bloody literal. He felt angry and he thought he shouldn't be, the gesture was kind. His father loved Annie. The daughter I never had, that's how he described her—his mouth always primed for cliché. Ellis found it hard to understand how flowers and care could reside equally in a man of such rage. Carol had tried to explain his father's complexity to him when he was younger. Piss off, he'd told her, the one and only time. I deserved that, she'd said, and never tried again.

Guilty. That's what he felt and that's why he was angry. He couldn't remember the last time he'd been there. He sat down on the ground even though it was damp. He placed the pink roses in the central urn and they looked unseasonably forced, their heads small and tightly held, still in shock, he thought, after the refrigerated journey from Holland. Her name on the stone still drew disbelief and sadness.

He used to find comfort planting flowers she'd like. He remembered he even had a theme once, only red flowers or variants thereof, until he realized the muntjacs were partial to a diet of bright petals. But he came and that was the most important thing. He faced the stark landscape of headstones and it was real. He would listen to people at Lewis's grave comment that he died on the same day as JFK, and they were right, he did. But Lewis's death was lost to the world as the world mourned Kennedy because sometimes you look away and things change. And every month or so, bright wreaths would adorn new graves and he would acknowledge the grieving. A reminder that he and they were not alone.

But then memories began to drift beyond his reach and the panic set in. He'd call people up whatever the time of night.

What did Annie cook when you came to dinner? he'd asked.

Ellis—d'you know what time it is?

What did she cook?

The phone went dead. Over time, the friendships too. Only Carol stayed on the line.

Ell?

He could hear the muffled sound of her getting out of bed.

What is it, Ell?

Annie. She used to sing a song when she was cooking and I don't know what it was. I don't know what it was, Carol, and I need to know—

Frank Sinatra, Ell. "Fly Me to the Moon."

"Fly Me to the Moon"!

She always went off-key in the middle—

Aw, she did, didn't she?

She was quite awful really, if you don't mind me saying.

Oh, she was.

D'you remember, Ell, when the six of us had dinner at the Italian place opposite Mabel's?

Sort of.

Your father stuck to beer because he couldn't pronounce the wine.

Ellis laughed.

I'm being naughty. Maybe it was your engagement dinner—

Yeah, I think it was.

You sat in the middle on one side. And—

Who was next to me?

Michael and Mabel. And me, your dad and Annie were opposite. They played a medley of Frank Sinatra songs. All the greats: "You Make Me Feel So Young." "I've Got You Under My Skin." "New York, New York"—that's when you told everyone you were going there for your honeymoon. And then they played—

—"Fly Me to the Moon," said Ellis. Annie stood up and she was drunk and she used the wine bottle as a microphone. And Michael joined her, didn't he?

Oh, they were so happy, Ell. So daft and so happy.

. . .

ELLIS STOOD UP and brushed the dirt off his trousers. He picked up his shopping and was about to walk away but stopped. He took one of the roses from the urn and went over and placed it on Lewis's grave. From my wife, he said, and he moved toward the churchyard gates.

He got off the bus at Gipsy Lane under a low sky suddenly threatening rain. The shopping bag was stretched taut and he wondered if it would split before he got it home. South Park was quiet and he could have gone for an early evening walk had it not been for the bag. He lifted it into his arms and picked up the pace.

He wasn't sure, at first, what it was in his front garden, part hidden by a bush. But when he got to the gate, he said, Hello, bike! and looked about for someone to thank. He walked on to Hill Top Road, down Divinity, but saw no one. An act of kindness from a stranger. He knelt to check out the chain and gears. Slight scuffing to the edge of the tire, that's all. He spun the front wheel and it rotated perfectly. He opened the front door and dropped the shopping bag on the table. He wheeled the bike into the hallway and left it at the bottom of the stairs. Later that evening, he brought it into the back room and placed it close to the fire.

．   ．   ．

DAYS WENT BY clearing the garden. Slow, one-handed
work that quietened his mind and had him rising with
intention. He ate breakfast outside, planning the day's
assault, the smell of early rain and mud curiously exhila-
rating.

Pruning shears he found in the garage. The floorboards
were there too, stacked up against the wall at the side of the
car. The smell of oak was sharp and fragrant still. He pulled
a plank away from the pile and turned it sideways to see
how straight it ran. He leaned his nose against the grain.
The smell of wood excited him, always had. He could still
lay the floor in the back room, he thought. He could get
back to working with wood. He was good, he was skilled,
they both said so. There are things I can do, he thought.

He brought a radio out to the garden and kept the volume low. He clipped away at the brambles inches at a
time and collected the cuttings in an old compost bag as he
went along. Jamie leaned across the fence and asked if he
needed any help. Ellis thanked him and said no, but later
Jamie brought him out a mug of strong tea and a plate of
biscuits, and he crept under the fence and sat on the bench
with him and they talked about rugby.

The stiffness in his wrist and elbow stopped him putting

in a full day's work and come the afternoon he walked what he called the tourist trail into town. Over The Plain and Magdalen Bridge, he cut through Rose Lane into the meadows and smoked a cigarette leaning against a storm-felled tree. Students jogged by and tourists dreamed, and as he got closer to the Thames, he had a sudden desire to be on the other side.

He crossed Folly Bridge, and the University boathouses shone golden in the last rays of the afternoon. The London train departing in the distance, geese, the slap of oars against water. These were timeless, familiar sounds to him.

He was drawn inexorably to the dark shadow of under-growth that was once Long Bridges bathing place, his and Michael's place, an ownership that extended well into adulthood. It had been closed these last years and he was surprised how quickly nature had advanced. Still attached to the concrete sides were the steps leading into the water but at the back the toilets were now roofless and filled with rubbish. It was hard to imagine they'd once called this place the Beach, but they had.

That first summer of their friendship, when the tem-perature nudged above seventy, they cycled down and squeezed themselves in between bodies on the grass. They sunbathed with arms behind their heads, and cooled off in the Thames's seductive flow. He remembered how Michael had bragged that he could swim, but he couldn't. He said that he'd read everything about swimming, firmly believing he could trip across words, like stepping-stones, to the bank of experience. But he couldn't. It would take another summer before Michael would learn to swim. But he floated, though. Facedown in the river with his arms and legs out wide, and people watched, and sometimes their laughter turned to panic when they saw little sign of movement. Dead man's float, he called it: a survival position after a long, exhausting journey.

And when the afternoon set down its long shadows, back on their bikes they got, still wet, still dopey, and with shirttails flapping, they dried out on the saddle in the breeze back to Mabel's. Summer's end they were sinewy and brown, and took up a little more space. Summer's end, they were inseparable.

Ellis looked up. Geese had taken flight toward Iffley and he watched their formation until they disappeared behind the trees. Dusk was creeping up fast and the ponds had turned black and the lowering sun gave way to a deceptive chill. He did up his jacket, stamped back across the damp grass to the bridge and towpath. At the dark edges, puddles shimmered as if starting to freeze and the flues from canal boats smoked generously. Up ahead, rock music blared out from the upper room of a boathouse. A solitary young man on a rowing machine kept stroke to the beat of the music. He was shirtless, his muscles distinct in the artificial light. Ellis stopped. He felt Michael's presence next to him, could almost smell him, the pronounced vagaries of longing. And he wanted to talk to him about the years they were apart because he hadn't during the months when he returned. Or those moments from youth, when they raced back to an empty room and nervously explored the other's body in a pact of undefined togetherness that would later bring him equal shame, equal joy. And those nine eventful days in France and the plans they made then—he'd let them go without acknowledgment, as if they'd never existed, or never been important to him and he never understood why. He had tried to talk to Annie once. She had asked him why he was so angry. She asked him things women ask men, things he wasn't able to talk about and he didn't know how to explain, not his confusion nor his discomfort. But he remembered her eyes were soft and open to him and they said, you can tell me anything, and he could have, he knew that even then. But he didn't. And now here he was, gazing at Beauty Rowing in the Darkness, as dog walkers passed by and students mistook his gaze for desire. All of it was important, he wanted to say. You were important to me, he wanted to say.

They used to come along here as men, often just the two

of them. Annie said they needed time together, she always
tried to give them time, especially after they were married.
She was the one who sensed things had changed, the one
who knew Michael was keeping secrets from them. When
did you last see him? she'd ask. About three weeks ago,
he'd say.

Jesus, Ell, you've got to do better with people.

He remembered how Michael and he walked the towpath to the ponds one particular day, and when they got
there, they both agreed so much had changed. It was only
March, but there was a quiet desolation to the place. Op-
portunistic flashers came down there now to wank. That's
what Michael said, his grin-sneer lighting up his face. Ellis,
however, remembered the desolation more a reflection of
their mood.

That was when Michael told him he was leaving Oxford. Ellis said, When? And Michael said, Soon. And he
said, Where are you going? And Michael said, Not far. Just
London. But you'll come back? Of course I will, said
Michael. Every weekend. How could I not?

And he did come back. Every weekend. Until Mabel
died, and then he didn't. He disappeared into the millions
of others who walked those crowded London streets, and
Ellis never knew why. He and Annie had an address, at

first, somewhere in Soho. But no matter what they sent out
the bird came back with nothing between its beak.

We have to stop this, said Annie one night. Go and
find him.

No, he said. Fuck him.

And that was that. A six-year standoff of wasted time.
His absence unbalanced them both in a way neither could
have predicted. Without Michael's energy and view of the
world they became the settled married couple both had
feared becoming. They made little demand of one another
and conversation gave way to silence, albeit comfortable
and familiar. Ellis withdrew, he knew he did. His hurt
turned to anger, there when he woke up and before he
slept. Life was not as fun without Michael. Life was not as
colorful without him. Life was not life without him. If only
Ellis could have told him that then maybe he would have
returned.

Five years they existed in this unfamiliar interlude, until
teenagers—bizarrely—prodded Ellis back to life. He was
in a café watching a group of them at a nearby table. They
were loud and comfortably draped across one another and
he enjoyed their gauche attempts at cool, at their more
charming traits of silliness. But it was their curiosity and
attentiveness that left an impression on him, the natural in-

terplay of their delight. And he wrote down on a scrap of paper what he observed about them, the qualities, the playfulness too, things he thought he'd relinquished in his relationship. He felt so grateful to them afterward that he went to the counter and quietly paid for them to have another round of coffee and cake.

Outside, as he passed the window, he saw their confusion and laughter as a laden tray was placed in front of them.

He went straightaway to a travel agency and got out the scrap of paper and asked for suggestions of a trip within three hours' flight of London. Included in this trip, however, had to be—and he read out loud—Delight. Wonder. Curiosity. Culture. Romance. Seduction.

That's easy, said the travel agent.

And a month later, they were in Venice.

The sudden impulse had them holding hands again across tables and leaping onto *vaporetti* that had already pulled away. And they holed up in a small hotel and breathed in the lagoon's old breath, and in the quiet corner of an *osteria* or sprawled across a bed with the thump of orgasm ripe in their throats, they found one another again.

One morning, they woke up to the flood siren and it was an eerie sound in the early hour. They got up and went outside. A skein of mist hung over the lagoon, the rising sun fiery and red and beautiful. The duckboards were out and they walked around dazed and took breakfast at the Rialto market, just a bun, but then they dared one another to have a glass of wine instead of an espresso, and it was perfect. And they walked. Siphoning information from passing tourist groups, resting against bridges in full sun, finding brief respite against the cold air, the soft slap of waves the city's musical pulse.

Spaghetti vongole was lunch, a dish that was a favorite, and they drank more wine and Ellis read out notes from a well-thumbed copy of *Venice for Pleasure*. Let's go back to the hotel, said Annie, smiling. In a bit, said Ellis. But there's a place we have to go to first, and he paid the bill and took her hand and they shared a slow amble toward San Rocco and into Tintoretto's beating heart.

In the Scuola Grande, they stood in awe as the Bible took shape and form above them and beside them. The beauty, the anguish of humanity startled them and silenced them. On the upper floor, Annie sat down on a chair and cried.

What is it? asked Ellis.

Everything, she said. This and having wine for breakfast and you and me and it's just everything. It's us. Knowing that we're OK and we can be silly too. He taught us silly, didn't he?

Ellis smiled. He did.

And I love you and we don't have to settle, do we?

We don't, he said.

And I do think of him still, you know, because I just want to know we're still important to him. I'm being selfish, I know. And Ellis said, I think about him too. And she kissed him and said, I know you do. We just love him, don't we?

They went back to the hotel and slept in Venetian dusk. They woke in the same position and opened their eyes to the sound of glasses clinking in the bar below. They went downstairs and sat at a table by the window. The cold sulked along the *calli* and gondoliers sang for tourists. A fire was lit in the hearth behind them and they held hands across the table and talked nonstop about unimportant things, and they laughed well together and they were the last to leave the bar. They undressed but didn't wash. They turned off the light and slept with their arms around one another. They said good-bye to a city reflected in a billion corrugations of water.

Three weeks later, Michael did come back to them as if he'd heard their lament across the sea. He walked in the same way he had walked out, with little explanation and that daft grin across his face. And, for a while, they became them again.

.   .   .

MUSIC FROM NEXT DOOR started early and it was loud. Ellis looked out onto their garden and saw three dustbins being filled with ice. It was bound to be an all-nighter, he thought, and he felt nervous. Christ, what the hell was he doing? Jamie had invited him earlier, tagged onto the end of an apology. Said something like, we're having a party tonight, Ellis. Sorry in advance for the noise. You're welcome to come if you want.

He stared at his limited array of clothes. Keep it simple, Annie would have said. Jeans, old Converse, light blue shirt. Socks or no socks? He looked at his ankles. Socks, he decided. He stepped back from the mirror, and ran his fingers through his hair. He hoped there'd be no dancing because then he'd have to leave.

The champagne had been in the fridge for a year or two, bought on a whim to elevate his mood, but he hadn't been able to face it because he never drank champagne alone, so it sat at the back of the fridge with a dark jar of pickled onions, which he had been afraid to open. He grabbed the bottle and walked out the back door. He squeezed through the hole in the bottom fence. He didn't know why he did that, he could have gone round to the front and rung the bell like any other normal person. He'd become feral and reclusive.

He found Jamie in the kitchen, and Jamie cheered when he saw him and said something like, Look who's here, folks! This is Ellis, everyone—All right, Ellis? Hi, Ellis. Nice to meet you, mate, etc. etc. The music was quite loud and Ellis had trouble understanding what people were saying to him. He smiled a lot and opened the champagne and moved back out to the garden with his new friends. He asked Jamie what the music was and he told him it was Radiohead, the song "High and Dry." He rarely listened to music anymore but he liked this music and thought he might even buy this music. Who is it again? he asked.

The champagne made him feel ridiculously bold (quickly drunk) and before he knew it, he had agreed to tell a joke and all these young eyes were on him. He thought for a moment.

He said, How do you make a snooker table laugh?

Pause.

Tickle its balls.

In the space after the punch line and before laughter, a brief silence ensued, in which he made plans to go home, watch television, that kind of thing, but then laughter erupted, and amidst the laughter people repeated the punch line and he was saved from an early night. A spliff was put in his hand and a refill of bubbles in the other, and Jamie leaned in close to his ear and told him he was really glad he

was there. And Ellis said he was too. And Jamie said he'd
won twenty quid in a bet. And Ellis said, What bet? And
Jamie said, Nobody thought you'd come. You're a mystery, mate.

The effect of the dope inched across his brain and he left
the crowds in the garden and went back inside to find a
quiet place to smoke in case he hallucinated. He was worried what might come out.

The front room was empty and blacked out, illuminated
solely by a television screen that emitted blue from a vast
blue ocean. He grabbed a cushion from the sofa, placed it
on the floor by the television and lay down. He looked up.
Dolphins were jumping over him. He smiled and inhaled a
lungful of thick sweet smoke.

She came into the room then. The door opened and she
stood in the doorway, a dark presence haloed by yellow
hallway light. She closed the door and sealed them in,
alone. He watched her move closer, too dark to see her
face, but her face became clear as she leaned over him and
asked if she could join him. He could smell her skin and it
could have been soap, or maybe the moisturizer she used,
but it was a heavenly smell. He thought she was pretty.
And much too young. She put a cushion down next to him
and took a smoke. They swapped names, and he forgot
hers straightaway because he was nervous, and he told her

all he knew about dolphins and their capacity for empathy, and she said, Uh huh, uh huh, and she leaned across him and blew smoke in his mouth. Her hair fell over him and smelled of pine. He was aware of her aliveness, the brutal honesty of her desire.

She put her hand on his chest and he thought his heart would explode, and he felt embarrassed because he knew she could feel it.

You look scared, she said, and laughed.

Sea otters now swimming in his eyes.

She undid his shirt buttons and her fingers played on his chest and she ran a fingernail down the hairline to his stomach, and the feeling was sublime and caused him pain, and he stopped her then and said, Enough now. He kissed her hand. Enough, he said.

OK, she said, and buttoned up his shirt. But can I rest my hand here, is that OK?

That's OK, he said, and he fell asleep with her hand on his chest and with tears spilling from the corners of his eyes.

It was morning. She had gone. He was lying alone on the floor of a strange room under a television with the lingering melancholy of a young woman's sweet touch. The house was quiet. He crept over bodies. In the hallway, the faint sound of lovemaking and snores gathered, and a quiet telephone conversation muffled by a hand. Through dark rooms the occasional light of a computer screen, or a portable television on mute. In the garden, the dustbins were full of water and empty bottles. He crawled back under the fence, a tomcat retreating home. He went straight to the bathroom and rinsed his face and hands, and his blue eyes stood out in the bloodshot whites. He came back downstairs and made an espresso in an Italian coffeepot he and Annie had brought back from Venice. In the bottom cupboard, he found an unopened pack of coffee beans and had to search for the electric grinder because like so many other things it had been pushed to the back.

He drank the coffee out in the garden as the garden awoke. He suddenly realized the clocks had gone forward and it was officially spring and the birds were loud because the birds knew. He undid his shirt and goose bumps rose. He rubbed his hand across the plaster cast, across the phone number written large in thick black pen. Across the words: "Call me. You're gorgeous. Love Becs."

THREE DAYS LATER, it was his father's birthday and he decided to make an effort. He'd bought him a new cap, a good cap, navy, and he'd bought it from Shepherd & Woodward on the High Street.

He gave him the present before the cake came out and his father said thank you and put the cap on immediately, and that's how Ellis knew he liked it. He adjusted it a little, moved the peak from side to side until it rested heavily on his ears. He sat at the table all cap and teeth and ears and Carol said, Suits you, Len.

She said, Show me the card now, and he held up his birthday card, a picture of an anxious-looking egg with the words, I'm cracking up, written above it.

That's funny, she said. What's it say inside? and he pushed the card across the table to her.

Happy Birthday Dad from Ellis, she said. She looked across at Ellis and mouthed, Thank you.

They sang Happy Birthday to him (he joined in near the end) and he blew out the candles with his cap on. There were seven candles for a man of seventy-six. Carol didn't explain why, it was probably all she had left in the drawer. Len cut his cake and Carol prompted him to make a wish, which he did, and Ellis thought, how is it possible I was afraid of this man?

They said little as they ate the cake, the sound of forks scraping against plates, the sound of glasses as toasts were made and beer was drunk. The room became hot and Ellis took off his sweater and Carol's eyelashes slapped against her cheek as she stared at his plaster cast.

Ellis instinctively rubbed his arm and said, It's just a joke, Carol. A mate wrote it for a joke. She doesn't exist.

Oh, Ell, she said, and she really did look disappointed. I thought—

I know, he said, quietly.

I really did think there was something you were going to tell us, she said.

There is, actually.

Go on, she said.

I've decided to leave work. For good, I mean. When this is off.

Silence.

The sound of the bloody clock. The sound of his father taking off his cap.

Oh, here we go, thought Ellis. (Bit tight now, would have been better in brown. What were you thinking? Still got the receipt?)

Just like that? said his father.

No. Not just like that. Ellis smiled. I've given it a lot of thought.

Who've you spoken to?

Bill McAuliffe. In personnel.

So it's official?

Yes.

His father finished his beer. It was a job for life, you know, he said.

I'll be fine, said Ellis.

What are you going to do?

The garden for the time being. One-handed of course, and he winked at Carol.

Gardening? said his father.

I find it peaceful.

His father scoffed and stared at his empty beer glass. And for money? he asked.

I still have Michael's, said Ellis.

Now you stop that, Leonard, said Carol, breaking the silence. He said he'll be fine and he'll be fine. You be happy for him now and that's an order. Put your cap back on. Be handsome again.

Ellis stood in the back garden, smoking. Lights from the Car Plant spilled across the darkening sky. He heard the back door open and close. Carol, of course. Smelled her before he could see her. He'd never asked them when the affair began but always presumed it ran along invisible tracks parallel to his parents' marriage. Mum had the painting and he had Carol. Truce.

I'm glad you're not going back there, she said. Some are

cut out for it, others aren't. I don't think you ever were, not really. You've been there a long time, Ell.

He nodded.

Too long, I reckon. I always said, When he behaves out of the ordinary, then I can stop worrying. It's hard being born here, breathing this air. It becomes part of you, whether you want it to or not. Those lights become dawn and dusk.

Mum used to say that.

Did she? We were friends once.

I never knew that.

In the early days, we were. But then she seemed to withdraw. Rarely went out with your dad anymore. Maybe it was being a new mum. I reckon you were enough for her. Lucky Dora, we used to say.

Ellis put his arm around her shoulder.

She said, I did try and get him to change his mind about school, all them years ago.

I know you did. I was always grateful.

It was hard for us, wasn't it? Getting to know each other?

We know each other now, said Ellis.

Yeah.

And you know you're too good for him.

I know, said Carol, and they laughed.

Do you think he's all right? said Ellis, looking back to the house.

Course he is. He's just used to being a bastard. He's one of them men who discovered later on that he's got a heart. Makes him a better dancer.

He dances?

When we go away he does. Won't do it round here in case anyone sees him. Says he's got a reputation to think about. What reputation? I say. Everyone's moved away. He's a nice little dancer. Takes it seriously, too. I reckon he thinks he's a little bit in the movies when he sweeps around. Are you happy, Ell?

Happy?

Christ! You say the word as if you don't know what it means.

I'm . . . hopeful.

Hopeful's a good word. You got a nice laugh, Ell.

Annie used to say that.

Life gets it wrong sometimes, doesn't it?

Did you find Mum's painting, by the way?

Oh God, course we did. We didn't get rid of it—

—No, I'm sure you didn't.

Let me go and ask your dad. He's in charge of things like that.

And she turned and went back toward the light of the kitchen.

A few minutes later, the back door opened again and his father appeared. Ellis watched him stumble across the lawn toward him, and thought his father looked like a boy in his new cap and his ill-fitting jacket, and he thought he looked so unsure of himself in this modern world because he saw none of it coming, not old age nor old thinking.

You all right out here? his father asked him.

Yeah. You warm enough?

Course. I've got a new cap. Wool, isn't it?

It is, said Ellis.

See you still smoke, then?

Yeah.

When did you start? Never asked you.

Nineteen? Twenty? Should stop, I know.

I started as a kid. Smoked the way others ate sweets.

Right.

I've asked Carol to marry me.

What? Just now?

No, said his father with a rare laugh. For the last twenty years. She's always said no.

Really?

Says she doesn't want me telling her what to do with her money.

And I thought she was just being modern, Ellis smiled.

Yeah, that too. But she said I had to get your permission first.

Mine?

So that's what I'm asking.

You have it.

You can think about it—

—Nothing to think about.

But you might feel different later.

I won't. Just marry her, Dad. Marry her.

His father took off his cap and smoothed his hair. He put the cap back on. Painting's upstairs, he said.

ON THE LANDING, Ellis pulled down the ladder and climbed up into the loft. He wasn't surprised by the tidiness or the order. Crawl boards splayed out in a grid system that made it easy to walk about, and boxes were neatly stacked with the contents written on the side: "Reader's Digest." "Shoes." "Bank Statements." He heard his father's voice below: I left it just inside. You can't miss it.

I *haven't* missed it! Oh, for fuck's sake, he said under his breath.

It's here. I've got it, he said loudly.

It was wrapped up in one of his mother's dresses. He

tugged the fabric away from the top right corner and the bowing head of a sunflower flashed out of the gloom.

I'm handing it down, he said. Here, he said, and his father reached up and took the painting from him. His father said, Don't forget the box as well. And Ellis said, What box?

And his father said, You'll see it. It's just inside to the left.

He turned to his left and saw it. A medium-sized cardboard box with "MICHAEL" written on the side.

CAROL PULLED UP outside the house. She helped Ellis inside with the painting and the box, and when he turned on the lights in the back room, he asked if she wanted a drink or a coffee.

No, she said. I won't stop, and she turned to go.

Carol?

What, love?

The box. Michael's things, he said. Why's he got it?

She paused. She said, You came to us after you cleaned out his flat. You don't remember, do you?

No.

You got back from London and stayed with us for weeks. You slept mostly. So we just kept the stuff with us.

Right.

It was difficult, Ellis. A very difficult time. Your dad thought it best to keep the status quo. What did he call that box? Pandora's box—that's it. He was worried that anything might set you off again. So we never mentioned it again. Just kept it up there. Did we do wrong?

No, course not—

If we did, I'm sorry—

You didn't.

But we don't have to worry now, do we?

No, you don't.

Carol buttoned up her coat. Said, It'll be strange not phoning you tomorrow, making sure you're OK. Won't know what to do with myself.

Ellis walked her along the hallway.

Come see us, she said. Don't be a stranger.

I won't. And he bent down and kissed her.

The front door shut. Silence now. The lingering smell of her perfume and lost, misunderstood years.

He uncovered the painting and leaned it against the wall. It was bigger than he remembered. And it was a fine copy, and deserved more than the incongruous fate of being a prize in a Christmas draw. The only signature on the front was "Vincent" written in blue. On the back, though, was the painter's signature: "John Chadwick." But who John Chadwick was, no one would ever know.

Fifteen sunflowers, some in bloom and some turning. Yellow on yellow pigment that darkened to ochre. Yellow earthenware vase decorated by a complementary blue line that cut across its middle.

The original was painted by one of the loneliest men on earth. But painted in a frenzy of optimism and gratitude and hope. A celebration of the transcendent power of the color yellow.

Nine years ago, in 1987, it sold for nearly twenty-five million pounds at Christie's auction house. His mum would have said, Told you so.

THE GARDEN took shape under April's eye. The flower-beds along the fence and walls of the house had been freed of weeds and transformed into perfect rectangles of tilled brown earth. Climbing roses and ivy were now supporting the crumbling back wall, and rhododendrons simply did their thing, flamboyant and loud in red and pink. He came across a family of primroses hidden under a nondescript shrub and transferred them to an area by the bench where he sat. He had grown to like primroses.

He stopped for lunch and ate outside. A plate of ham that he didn't need to cut, just folded it into his mouth with a fork. He remembered a time when he didn't like to be in this garden. He thought he had punished it, secretly, for being the last place he had spent time with them. He chose not to go further with those thoughts that day, and began to peel a boiled egg. A blackbird joined him on the arm of the bench. It had followed him around the garden most of the morning and made him think about the possibility of getting a pet.

By late afternoon, he had showered and had decided to walk across to South Park. The grass was newly mowed, the scent sweet, and those towering spires glinted to his left. The sun was beginning to dip, but there was still warmth, and the light, he thought, beautiful. He stopped where the three of them used to watch the fireworks display every autumn. Where they used to hand around a small flask of Scotch as lights above them flickered and cascaded across their cold, delighted faces. Where afterward, they'd tramp across the dewy grass and Michael would complain about his feet, and they'd make their way to the Bear smelling of bonfire and earth. The three of them, breath misting, trying to walk in sync. Left, right, left, right. Keep up, Ell, you're fucking it up!

Everywhere he went he knew they had gone before.

He stopped. He became aware that he had inadvertently stumbled into a scene of romance. Up ahead, a young man was leaning toward a tree, and from this tree, arms reached out and draped about his neck. He didn't want to ruin their moment of privacy, so he decided to pass through but not to look, and as he moved toward them he speeded up.

And yet, it was instinctive, his turn. Because the outline of the person leaning against the tree was so familiar to him, and so it was instinctive for him to turn and say, Billy?

Billy froze. Across his face settled the shame of discovery, and his words were quiet. All right, Ellis, he said. And Ellis didn't want it to be like that, not for Billy and his nineteen years, so he smiled and went toward him and said, Is this Martyrs' Memorial, then?

And Billy said, Yeah, and he looked up. Yeah.

Ellis turned to the young man and offered his hand, said, Good to meet you. I'm Ellis. I worked with Billy, and the young man said, I'm Dan.

How's life, Billy?

All right.

Work?

Not the same. I'm still on nights and it messes with my head. I don't know how you did it, Ell.

I know.

You're not coming back, are you?

No.

Fuck it, Ell. You let me down. I should've heard it from you, not from that fucking twat Glynn. You have to do better with people.

I'll do better.

It's no fun being your friend. Jesus.

And I'm keeping your tools, he added.

Ellis smiled. You should. Garvy gave them to me, I give them to you. It's continuity, right?

What are you going to do?

I don't know yet, said Ellis.

You should get away.

You reckon?

Yeah. Take a gap year.

Ellis laughed. OK.

Billy? said Dan, quietly.

I know. We've gotta go.

Yeah, yeah. Go.

Billy took out a pen and quickly scribbled on a scrap of paper. There's my number, he said. Call me sometime.

I will, said Ellis.

They left in opposite directions. Ellis was almost at the gate when Billy shouted out his name. He turned. There he was with his arm raised high. Follow the Yellow Brick Road, Ell!

.   .   .

FOLLOW, FOLLOW, FOLLOW, FOLLOW, Annie and
Michael sang arm in arm along Hill Top Road. June 1978.
Two weeks before the wedding. Michael had organized the
stag and hen and had merged them into one. Travel light,
he'd said. Flip-flops, shorts, that type of thing. Ellis
watched them up ahead. The doors to Mabel's van were
open and Michael had unfolded a large map that the breeze
was lifting. He heard Annie ask, So where are we going,
Mikey?

Not telling, he said, and he refolded the map and threw
it under the seat. All aboard, please, he said. Last one in's a
sissy.

Ellis jumped into the back, last.

Sissy, they said.

Music, please, copilot, said Michael.

Annie bent down and put the cassette player on her lap.
Michael handed her a tape. "Road Trip Mix" on the label.
She put the tape into the machine and pressed play: "He-
roes," David Bowie. They screamed. They wound down
the windows and sang out loud into summer dusk as the
familiar roads of Headington slipped away behind them.
Michael accelerated onto the A40, and the old van shook
with effort and weight.

Through Eynsham, Burford, Northleach.

They listened to Blondie, Barry White, Donna Summer.

Through Bourton on the Water, Stow on the Wold.

They listened to Abba.

In the middle of "Dancing Queen," the van changed direction but Ellis didn't say anything. He leaned forward and put his hands on Michael's shoulders. And during "Take a Chance on Me," he did something unusual and sang the solo whenever Agnetha someone sang the solo. At the end of the song, he said, Garvy taught me that.

And they cried, Garvy! Garvy! Garvy! and the old van shook as if it was laughing.

The sky was losing light and Ellis noticed Michael glance at his watch. Soon the recognizable cityscape of home came back upon them.

Mikey? said Annie.

Mikey looked at her and grinned.

They returned through Summertown, through St. Giles. Don't say a word, he said, and they obeyed. Looked out at the University buildings, illuminated and grand, at the pubs with students congregating outside.

Michael pulled up in Magdalen Road. They followed him into the shop and through to the back. The kitchen was dark and silent and Michael opened the back door. They walked out into a garden lit by scores of candles masquerading as stars. And in the middle of this constellation, two tents side by side, and behind the tents a large paddling pool where a lone boat floated with a tealight on its hull. It was simple, it was daft, it was beautiful, it was Michael.

Let me show you to your room, he said, and he walked them to the larger tent. Inside were sleeping bags zipped together. May I suggest a swim in the lake tomorrow? he said. Weather permitting, of course.

They changed immediately into denim cutoffs and flip-flops. The evening was cool, so jumpers hid T-shirts and Ellis built a fire in a ring of bricks. They all turned to look as the back door opened.

Ah, said Michael. Here comes the gypsy of the old fen, the Lighter of Lights.

What's that? said Mabel, holding a bottle of champagne.

The deaf gypsy of the old fen, said Michael.

Go on with you, she said, and she opened the champagne, which took a while, and Ellis handed around mugs stained with tea and they drank from these mugs and they toasted three times.

To you two! said Michael.

To us! said Annie.

For nothing to change, said Ellis.

And that was the night Michael ran across the road to the Italian restaurant and brought back plates of *spaghetti vongole*, which no one had ever tasted before. A bottle of red wine, too, Chianti Ruffino in a basket. This is fancy, said Mabel.

The next morning, he and Annie awoke to the sound of rain. They dozed and huddled close as the damp crept in. They heard the sound of the back door open, flip-flops running across the grass.

Knock knock, said Michael. Coffee! And he tugged the zip down and his beaming face filled the space.

Look how handsome he is, said Annie.

It's unbearable, said Ellis.

Budge up, said Michael, water dripping down his forehead. One cappuccino and two espressos, he said. The Italian pastries in his pocket, miraculously dry.

They settled down to a morning of Scrabble, speeding up the game with double points for dirty words, which Ellis won. Lunchtime, the gypsy of the old fen came out with sausage sandwiches, and afterward the clouds broke up and the sun cast hazy rays toward the earth and the tents began to steam. Annie helped Mabel off with her shoes, and together they went for a paddle, and Mabel said, All this, and we're still in Oxford.

I'm going to light the candles again tonight, said Ellis.

Do it, said Michael.

And when light fell, the constellations flickered, and

Ellis sat in the pool with a wooden boat rocking by his foot. The boat capsized when Annie and Michael got into the water.

I don't ever want to settle, said Ellis, looking from one to the other.

I won't let you settle, said Annie.

And I won't let you settle, and Michael handed him a mug of champagne.

Ellis drank. Where are we again? he said, looking around.

Greece, said Annie. An island called Skyros.

The fishing boats are coming in, said Michael. Look. You can see their lights coming to shore.

So what's the plan for tomorrow? said Ellis.

More of the same, said Annie. Stay on the beach. Maybe a cycle around the island, later. We don't want to overdo it, do we? We've got so much time.

IT WAS MAY DAY, and students still had flowers in their hair. Ellis's cast was off and he cycled through town and down St. Aldate's to the river. The sun had come out for the first time that afternoon and the towpath was busy.

He turned off into Long Bridges where the river was still, where an occasional breeze rippled the surface when he wasn't looking. He moved away from the bridge toward the concrete bank hidden by a thick hedge of brambles, and there he undressed. He was shy at first. He sat on the side with his feet in the water and his hands in his lap. A shout from a rowing cox the other side of the trees, and the thump of blades slicing the river was the sound of Oxford in spring. The fleeting glimmer of bikes speeding along the path to his left. He slipped into the cold water and his nakedness felt electrifying. Mud squeezed between his toes, and he half-expected to feel the familiar flicker of minnows around his ankles as he used to do. He swam in the wake of a mallard and felt the pleasure of the sun breathing hard on his arm. As he swam, a memory came to him. The last summer with his mother, it would have been. He could see her again, lying among the crowds on the opposite bank, and she was laughing. She had just asked Michael what book he was reading and he held it up and said, *Leaves of Grass* by Walt Whitman. He said they were doing the American Civil War at school and they had to present something to class about Abraham Lincoln. He had chosen to do a poem about Lincoln's death. It wasn't easy, he said. And the book had been banned, once, on account of its sexual content.

That's what had set his mother off laughing. Sexual

content? she said. Did Mrs. Gordon at the library tell you that?

She's a liberal educationist, he said.

Really? A liberal in Cowley? And pigs might fly.

It's a poem about grief, he said.

Grief? she repeated. And then she said, Are they ready for you, Michael?

For my recital?

No, she said. Are they ready for you? Is the world ready for you?

He smiled and said, I'm not sure, and he began to read the poem out loud to her, hitting the last word of every sentence, to make sure she heard the rhyme.

> O Captain! my Captain! our fearful trip is done;
> The ship has weather'd every rack, the prize we
>   sought is won;
> The port is near, the bells I hear, the people all
>   exulting,
> While follow eyes the steady keel, the vessel grim
>   and daring . . .

And Ellis remembered thinking he would never meet anyone like him again, and in that acknowledgment, he knew, was love. He could see his mother concentrating on Michael's words, how enraptured she was. And when he stopped, she bent down and kissed him on the head and said, Thank you. Because everything she held on to and everything she believed in came together in that unexpected moment. The simple belief that men and boys were capable of beautiful things.

His mother stood up and all eyes were upon her. She walked down to the river and climbed down the steps until she was mid-waist in water. Michael ran after her and said, Dora! Pretend to save me from drowning, and he jumped in and swam out to the middle of the pond with his arms and legs kicking and flailing. And there he waited for her, ignoring the laughter that came from the side. And his mother did it. She swam over to him and silenced people's ridicule. She calmed him, told him not to panic, and she reached under his arms and gently pulled him the length of the pond through dappled light and ripples. And all the way, Michael quoted,

> O Captain! my Captain! rise up and hear the bells . . .

Ellis lifted himself out of the water and sat on the side. He covered his lap with a T-shirt, conscious of the possible appearance of children, and he dried off in the sun. He closed his eyes and his body softened. He wondered again why he hadn't gone to the talk with them that long-ago evening. And he didn't push the thought away as he usually did, but he stayed with it, listened to it because it couldn't hurt him today, not there.

It was a book talk, that's all, about what? He still couldn't remember. They hadn't even stayed for the duration, that's why they were found out near Binsey. Annie loved to drive out there, that's how he knew it was her idea and not Michael's. Oh, Annie. Bad idea. Bad.

He remembered how the floorboards had just been delivered and he sat out in the garden with a beer, looking up at the sky, noticing its stillness, thinking how beautiful it would have been to be in a plane right then, the three of them again, heading toward a new horizon. He remembered music that night—Chet Baker, trumpet not vocals—and he remembered thinking how lucky he was to love them. That he should've had such a thought used to wake him up in a sweat.

That was the world he inhabited between the time of it happening and the time of him knowing. A brief window, not yet shattered, when music still stirred, when beer still tasted good, when dreams could still be hatched at the sight of a plane careering across a perfect summer sky.

The doorbell rang and he thought it was them, but it couldn't have been them, could it? Because they each had a key. He opened the door and the policemen seemed too young to bring bad news, but they did. They walked him into the front room, where time evaporated. He thought he'd blacked out, but he hadn't. It was life as he knew it shutting down.

They drove him to the hospital. There were no sirens or flashing lights, there was no hurry because it was all over. Annie looked peaceful. A bruise around her temple, stupid really, that that's all it took. And when he told the nurse he was ready to see Michael she said that the doctor would be along in a minute. He sat and waited in the corridor with the policemen. They got him a cup of tea and a Kit Kat.

The doctor led him to an empty room where he told him Michael had been taken to the morgue. Ellis said, Why? Is that normal? And the doctor said, Under the circumstances it's normal. What circumstances? said Ellis.

We found a cluster of lesions down his right side. Kaposi—

—I know what they're called, said Ellis.

Michael had AIDS, he said.

I don't think so, said Ellis, and he reached for a cigarette but the fucking doctor told him he couldn't. He would've told me, he said.

He walked out into the night and he wanted to speak to someone but there was no one left. His father and Carol were waiting for him at the front gate. Talk to me, Carol kept saying. Talk to me. But he never did.

He scattered Michael's ashes down by his favorite stretch of river, as per instructions. He was alone. The wind bit hard across the meadow. It was the end of summer.

DUSK WAS FALLING. Ellis sat out in the garden under a blue sky streaked with gold and lilac. Jazz played from next door. The students had borrowed his collection of Bill Evans, and they were cooking. The kitchen door was open and he could hear the clash of pans, beer bottles being opened, and the murmur of a recipe. He liked to listen to them, he had grown fond of their ways.

He felt cold after the swim. He hadn't yet showered and he went back inside to get a jumper. It was on the armchair by the fire, and he put it on immediately. He stopped in front of his mother's painting and wondered, as he so often did, what she'd been looking for. He found the painting peaceful, so could it have been as simple as that? Peace? He didn't think so, but some mornings, when light fell on the canvas, the yellow did something to his head. Woke him up, made him feel brighter. Was that it, Mum? Was it? He turned round and caught his foot on the cardboard box he'd brought back from his father's. He knelt down. When? he said to himself. If not now, then when?

He tore the tape away from the top and the brief glimpse of a shirt made him draw breath. He picked up the box and took it outside to the bench. He came back and grabbed a half-opened bottle of wine from the fridge and a glass that lived on the draining board. He sat in the garden and waited for his nerves to settle.

He had no idea what he'd kept or what he'd jettisoned all those years ago. What he never forgot, though, was his shock at how little Michael had owned. One chair. A radio. A few books. His flat was a lonely space or a clever space. Minimalist to the extreme. It was a place of contemplation not distraction. A place of thought.

He lifted the clothes from the box and placed them on his lap. The pale blue T-shirt he and Annie got him from New York, the neckline frayed because he never took it off. Ellis held it up to his nose and didn't know what to expect, the only smell was a faint trace of washing powder lifting the must. A white linen shirt, a navy cashmere sweater, miraculously untouched by moths. A striped Breton top wrapped around a copy of Whitman's *Leaves of Grass*. On the inside cover "The Property of Cowley Library" had been crossed out and replaced with the name "Michael Wright."

Across the fence, "My Foolish Heart" played for the second time that evening. Ellis poured out the wine and drank.

From the box, he brought out a large envelope that he emptied beside him. A mix of ephemera from a drawer, that's what it looked like. Torn-off images from magazines, a crumpled black-and-white photograph of him and Michael caught off guard at a bar in France looking sun-bronzed, nineteen? and rightfully invincible.

Another photo, this one of him and Annie on their wedding day, staring at clouds of confetti as if it was cherry blossom instead. An invitation to an art opening in Suffolk—Landscapes by Gerrard Douglas. A color photograph of Mabel and Mrs. Khan outside the shop, the day Mrs. Khan came to work there. Testament to a rare friendship that spanned nearly thirty years. They are wearing brown aprons and their arms are around one another, and they are looking at the camera and smiling. Mabel's white hair has been set by rollers as it always was, her cheeks colored by the simple joy of living. She would never retire. What's the point of that? she always used to say. And now postcards—Henry Moore, Francis Bacon, Barbara Hepworth. A folded newspaper, an *Oxford Times* dated 1969. He was about to put it to one side when he realized it was the first article Michael had ever written. It was about Judy Garland.

The day she died, Ellis remembered, Michael played the Carnegie Hall album. He opened the shop door and turned the volume up high. It was his way of honoring her. People came in to listen and Mabel gave out medicinal sherry and something stronger for the regulars. Afterward, Michael begged the *Times* to let him write something, to get away from making tea and making copy, and in the end he wore them down and they agreed he could write about Garland as long as there was Oxford interest too. And he found someone in Summertown who had been to the concert itself in '61, and he based the article around that—local interest combined with global phenomena—the lifelong fan who would now transfer her affection to the daughter. It was something, wasn't it? Center of the Universe, this shop, Michael used to say. Oh, we were. We were.

Another photograph, but this one of a man he didn't know standing next to an easel. He is wearing shorts and his chest is covered in paint. He is smiling. On the easel is a portrait of Michael. On the back of the photograph the letter "G."

A postcard of van Gogh's *Sunflowers*. A memory of his

mother or someone else? A phone number scrawled on the reverse. Cinema stubs—*Cinema Paradiso*, *Stand by Me*, *Pretty in Pink*—a ticket to Michael Clark, a ticket to the Tate/Turner Prize 1989.

From the bottom of the box, he took out a handful of books and instantly recognized them. They were his sketchbooks, the ones from childhood. And he couldn't believe he was looking at them again because he often threw them out when the pages were full, because nothing felt good enough, or so he thought then. Only one person thought they were good enough and he'd fucking saved them. Michael had saved them. He'd gone to those bins and pulled them out and kept them across the years.

Here was his mother. A simple line drawing of her profile, no shading, just a line running from her hairline down her nose and throat. Pages of this exercise until he got it right. Her hands now, pages of hands. And a watercolor of her face pretending to sleep, the curl of a smile at her upper red lip.

Ellis picked up another book: Michael. How old was he? Fourteen? Fifteen, maybe. Jeans low and shirt off and barefoot. Fingers around his belt loops, brooding and serious. Make me look interesting, he used to say. Make me look like a poet.

Oh Jesus. Ellis sat back and closed his eyes. He listened

to a conversation about olive oil coming from next door. He drank wine and poured out more. When he was ready, he picked up another book. Inside, though, he found words not drawings, and the sight of Michael's writing startled him. It wasn't a diary, it looked more random than that— thoughts, ideas, doodles. November 1989, it began, the time they were apart.

He began to read. There was a momentary flutter of the page, maybe the breeze or a tremor from his hand. A young man's voice traveled across the fence.

Ellis? he said. Ell?

But Ellis didn't hear. "November 1989," he read. "I don't know the day, the days have become irrelevant."

MICHAEL

November 1989

I don't know the day, the days have become irrelevant. G's sight has failed, and I've become his eyes. When he howls in the night I don't let go of him. The virus has entered his brain. Yesterday, he laughed when he pissed against the bedroom door.

A DOCTOR SUGGESTED I write to make sense of the world around me. There is no sense, I said, abruptly.

Witnessing the agony of others, he continued, the bewilderment of others. What do you think this has done to you?

I took my time with this absurd question. I'm not so fun anymore, I said.

He wasn't really a doctor doctor but a psychiatrist who

works with the dying. I'm not dying, it must be said. Not yet, anyway. I have a visualization tape and the cheery American voice tells me my body is full of light and *lurve* and I believe it. I'm so full of light and love, in fact, I can hardly do my trousers up. There's a line of fat around my belly that wasn't there a few weeks ago, and my abs used to be harder, too, more defined. If I was describing myself, I'd say this body has seen better days.

I'm thirty-nine years old, nearly forty. Does this bother me? I say it quickly when people ask, so it probably does. I don't smoke anymore, nor do I take drugs (apart from the occasional co-codamol that I stockpiled after G went onto IV). I used to be good-looking—this isn't vanity speaking, I was actually told that a lot—but I'm not sure I am anymore. People do still look at me and I get the odd suggestion at times (sometimes very odd), so maybe I still have something. Men liked to fuck me and liked me to fuck them. I had my standards. I dropped them on occasion, but generally I've been consistent. I liked short-term lovers or my own company. I've had really good lovers—inventive, exciting—but I was never one myself. I was a 7 max. I was the fantasy that rarely delivered. The slight hint of melancholy as they zipped up their trousers. I think I was a bit selfish. Or lazy. A 7, max. That was me.

My penis looks wistful, but it may be the light. In fact,

I'm sure it was bigger once. But I was skinny and skinny men always look as if their cocks are big. It's all just proportion really, and I've seen enough to know. Anyway, it's been bigger and that's because I'm teetering on the abyss of impotence and that ache, that throbbing—whatever you want to call it—well, it's gone. And that's OK. I like reflexology now because it helps me sleep.

Enough for today. The medication alarm has gone off and I need to check on him. I call him G because he never liked his name. He's not my boyfriend anymore. He's twenty-six and alone.

IT'S LATE. I've made vegetable broth. G's sleeping and his temperature is 99.5. He's burning up but he's got no sweats as yet. I'm not panicking because we've been here before. He's all bone, a T-cell count of zero. What keeps him alive, God only knows, the memory of living, I suppose. Every victory over infection we've celebrated, only to be dumped by a wave of despair a week or so later, as the mercury rose again. I know if he goes into hospital he won't come out, but we said our good-byes long ago. The morphine drips and I whisper sweet everythings to him. I watch the digital clock flick over. At 21:47 all is calm.

Autumn knocks on the window. I pull back the sliding

doors and let it in. Lights from the meat market flicker and car lights streak the gloom. Overhead the pulse of airplane wings replaces the stars. The flat is quiet. This is loneliness.

I used to write for a living. Maybe that's why I have an aversion to it now. I was a journalist. Started with local press, then freelance. Eventually, I turned to publishing and became an editor. Fiction mainly. I was suited to this because I was good at altering the story. Well, that's what someone said to me once. At the time, I'm not so sure it was a compliment.

I've stopped working for money. I have money. I'm not rich but I've enough for my needs. I get a carer's allowance and buy things that bring pleasure—flowers, a decent-quality steak, that sort of thing. I make sure we eat well, or did, I should've said because G's back on the liquid stuff. Ensure, it's called—silly name. I mix it with ice cream, and used to get the good stuff. Organic with natural vanilla. I don't do that now because he doesn't keep it down.

I can't do deadlines when everyone is dying. I actually wrote that on my resignation letter. How grand was I? I thought it captured the mood of the day, a mix of the political, the desperate, the personal. Eventually, I put down the wineglass and redrafted. Said something simple like, Time to move on and maybe write? and my publishers understood without asking me more. I worked out my notice and slipped away with a box of books I'd helped to get onto the shelves. Not one was my story, though.

G was an artist when we met. Five years ago now, not long after Mabel's death. I was sheltering in the National Gallery one rainy afternoon when I noticed him in the crowd, his resemblance to Ellis staggering—kind eyes, that hair, beard waiting to break out—and I followed him for two hours across an eclectic journey of Titian, Vermeer and Cézanne, until we ended up in front of a painting that had come to embody an important part of my childhood. I stood behind him, and in my most sonorous voice, said: He painted it in Arles in 1888, you know. As an act of gratitude. Friendship. And hope.

He laughed. You're creepy, he said and walked on. He was right. I'm not a natural cruiser. Have been told that many times before.

I followed him down to the bookshop and picked up books I had no intention of reading and looked at postcards I wasn't going to buy. Come on, he said as he passed me at the door, and we went to a café just off St. Martin's Lane, and after two double espressos and a slab of chocolate torte the embarrassing age gap between us diminished and I'd persuaded myself it was almost respectable. He asked me where I lived and I said, Soho, not far. Let's go, he said.

Really? I said. But I'm not having sex with you, he said. You're not the first to say that, I said. I've got jet lag, he said. So we can have tea, I said.

We didn't have sex but we did have tea. He slept and I watched him. And then I slept and woke up alone. A postcard of van Gogh's *Sunflowers* on my pillow, a phone number scrawled on the back. I called him that evening, left a message from Vincent on his answer machine, something about a lost ear. Four days later I was on a train.

He lived in a barn out in Suffolk, rented it off a couple of queens who spent most of their days in France. Friday nights, he'd ride with another bike by his side and meet me at Woodbridge station and we'd cycle the short distance back to his studio barn, where I'd unpack my rucksack and lay out the spoils of our weekend on the rough oak floor—the wine, the food, a video maybe, and the latest manuscript I was working on.

His body was a landscape of angles and valleys, a line of dark hair from his navel exploding around his penis, a light dusting of fuzz across his chest and buttocks. He made me feel who I'd been all those years ago with Ellis—who am I kidding? He reminded me of Ellis and not just in looks but how intense he was, how hidden, and I became the boy I'd once been, living out the fantasy of a long-gone youth.

I could watch for hours as he ground chunks of solid

paint pigment and mixed it with oil before scooping it into open-bottomed tubes. He made me calm. Made me learn the names of paints, and I told him that Scarlet Lake and Rose Madder would be our drag queen names, should circumstance ever force us onto the stage.

Summer light shone in. Pollen dust diffused the scene, the scent of flowers, smells of linseed and coffee, brushes standing in olive cans, wildflowers too. A paint-splattered bed in the corner and me making martinis naked, as G painted an abstract aberration of light across a field. It was everything Ellis and I had once planned. It was beautiful and, occasionally, it hurt. I told G that, and he laughed and the fantasy ended.

Did I love him? Yes, although I hesitate to use the word, because it turned very parental after a while, and after a while I encouraged him to see other men. I think he was grateful, certainly the bohemian in his soul was. But I wasn't being generous or open-minded. It was a friend I needed then, nothing more. Eventually, we became the two ends of a telephone line, same time every week. Yes? I'd say. What now? I'd say. What grubby adventure have you got up to this week?

Eighteen months ago, the phone rang. Yes? I said. What now? I said. What—

But there was silence.

G?

Silence. He began to cry.

Talk to me, I said. Silence.

I've got it, he said. It: the shorthand we all understood.

I said I'd never leave his side.

HE'S AWAKE NOW and he's shouting and it's three in the morning. What's happened to us, G? I can't cope anymore.

I telephone Barts and they'll have a bed ready for him, they say. I strap him into the chair and cover him with blankets and he shits two minutes after leaving the flat. The lift stinks and I know there'll be another anonymous note put through the door. Outside, fresh air and no rain. I hurry down Long Lane past the hum of refrigerated lorries into the smoke and chat of the meat porters. I put my hand on G's shoulder for reassurance. He's quiet now and calm. I see our reflection in the restaurant window. We are a still life. *Me and Old Man*. Fuck.

THE WARD IS KIND and they know us. We're on first-name terms with the doctors and nurses, which is good but also bad because it shows how many times we've been here.

The rooms are private with private bathrooms, thank God. There are no masks, no gloves, no rules, no visiting hours because this is a ward of palliative care. Temperatures are meticulously read, every two, four hours, to monitor the progression of infections, and days are measured out in the monotony of medication. Many contemplate suicide and refuse to eat. They're not force-fed, but are allowed to drift off slowly to that sought-after end. Our dead are placed in body bags, as any blood-borne virus would be, and are whisked off pretty sharpish to the morgue, where a sympathetic funeral director comes by and looks on with unprejudiced care. Many of the nurses are male and many are gay. They've volunteered to work this ward specifically. I can't imagine what they must be thinking, the young ones especially.

I used to wonder how it would be if I left G here and never came back. Didn't have to strip a soiled bed again, or flush out a chest port again, just left him here for good. Be done with it all, for good. I could never do it, though, could I? Once, in the throes of passion, I'd declared I'd do anything for him. So this now, this is my anything for him. How shy our bodies are now, G. How sad we are. He likes me to comb his hair because he remembers when he was still handsome. I do it. And I tell him he's still handsome.

I turn off his light and tell him I'll see him tomorrow.

I leave the telephone number of his parents for the ward to deal with because I've never been able to get through to them. Metaphorically speaking, that is. I go home and sleep for hours.

TWO DAYS AGO, just along the corridor from G's room, I met a young man. He heard me outside his room and called me in. I hesitated in the doorway, taken aback, momentarily, by the yellow autumn light that had fallen across his bed. He was full-blown with a sarcoma down the side of his nose and he was losing his hair from the chemo. He smiled.

He told me his name was Chris and that he was twenty-one years old and that his parents believed he was still backpacking around Asia. In the quiet space that followed that declaration, I picked up a chair and sat next to his bed. I asked him where his two friends were, the young man and woman I'd seen hovering by the door a couple of days before.

Gone back to Bristol, he said. Is that where you're from? I said. Yes, he said. I said I liked Bristol and he said he would've liked it better if he'd met me there. I laughed. I asked him if he was flirting with me and his eyes became bright. I'll take that as a yes, I said.

He asked me why I was here and I told him about G.

The shortened version, of course. Everyone's story is the same.

He told me he'd been encouraged by a doctor to write a letter to his parents. He lifted his right hand and it was red and swollen and he asked me if I'd help him do it. I said I would. I asked if he wanted to start the letter right away, but he said no. Tomorrow would be fine.

Tomorrow came and we got no further than "Dear Mum and Dad."

Today, though, we have made better progress and when the sadness overwhelms him, I put down the pen, and begin to rub his feet. Reflexology is the new sex, I say. He looks at me incredulously. Humor me, I say. His feet are cold and he smiles as I touch him. Does this mean we're going steady? he says, and I say, Oh, yes, you're all mine, and his smile leads to a not-so-distant boyhood, which completely disarms me.

Hand me my wallet, he says, and I do what he asks. Open it, he says. There's a passport photograph just inside. It's not very good, he says.

They never are, I say, as I take out the picture.

Two years ago, he says. I was nineteen.

I've seen that sort of change before and my face no longer registers shock. Clear skin, thick blond hair, downy chin. Glasses.

You're lovely, I say.

Not really, he says. But my hair'll grow back, and—

Shall I get us some tea? I say, a sudden need to leave the room.

I wasn't promiscuous, he declares.

I stop. Ambushed by his quiet defense against the disease, the bigots, the press, the Church.

I think I know the person, he says. You do, don't you? Looking back. That's what someone told me. Do you believe that?

I'm not sure what I believe, I say, sharply. No one deserves to go through this. That's all I know. You're lovely.

I leave the room. I take my rage out on the kettle and cutlery drawer. The nurses can hear me make the tea, fucking London can hear me make the tea. Onto a plate, I pile biscuits that I don't even feel like eating, and return to his room.

How are you with food? I ask him.

Not too good right now, he says.

These are mine then, I say, and I sit down and place the chocolate bourbons on my lap.

You'll get fat, he says.

I am fat, and I lift up my jumper. This wasn't here yesterday, I say. This is trespassing.

He laughs. Have you ever been in love? he asks.

I look at him and roll my eyes and immediately wish I hadn't.

I haven't, he says. I would've liked to.

It's overrated, I say, stuffing biscuits into my mouth. I eat through the silence, stuffing and eating, because I know I've done something wrong.

Don't do that to me, he says.

Do what? I say.

Make out things are nothing. Things that I'm not going to experience. That's fucked up. Pity you if you thought it was overrated. I would've fucking reveled in it.

I stand up, admonished, my feelings disengaged. A pathetic creature with biscuit crumbs stuck to his jumper.

You can go now, he says, turning away from me. And close the door, will you?

I do as he asks. I go to G's room and need him to comfort me, but he's asleep and dying. I'm fucked up. I leave.

HOME. I'VE OPENED the windows and the cold London air streams in, and with it comes the incessant sound of sirens and traffic, sounds I've grown to love. Candles burn on tabletops and the scent of tuberose surrounds me. Sometimes in this perfumed haze, I forget hospitals. Just sometimes, with a glass in my hand, I walk past a flame and its goodness replenishes me. I don't want to be defined by all this. We were all so much more than this once.

I pour out the wine. I think about Chris and how I behaved with him. I try hard to be liked, I always have. I try hard to lessen people's pain. I try hard because I can't face my own.

I sit wrapped up in a blanket on the balcony. I feel cold but cold is good because the ward is hot. Propped up on my knees is a black-and-white photograph. Me and Ellis in a bar in Saint-Raphaël in 1969, drinking pastis. We were nineteen. I remember how the photographer went around bars at night and handed out his card. You could go and look at the photographs in his studio the next day, and I did. Ellis thought it was a con so I went by myself. I saw this photograph as soon as I walked in, my sight completely drawn to where it was pinned amidst dozens of others. It's agonizing how beautiful we are.

Tanned faces and Breton tops, we'd been in France for five days already, and felt like locals. We went to the same bar each night down on the beach. A broken-down shack that sold sandwiches during the day and dreams at night. Well, that's what I used to say, and Ellis would squirm but he liked it really, I know he did. The bit about dreams. Who wouldn't?

In the captured moment, we say *Salut! Salut!* and touch

glasses, and the smell of aniseed rises sweet and inviting. Hey! a man's voice makes us turn. FLASH! Eyes blinded momentarily, our backs against the bar. We squint. A business card is thrust into my hand. The photographer says, *Demain, oui?* I smile. *Merci*, I say. It's a con, whispers Ellis. You're a bloody con, I say.

The smell of grilled octopus lured us out onto the terrace, an area of hessian matting that gave way to the sand. We stood looking out over an unstirring black sea that merged seamlessly with night. Lights from fishing boats swayed elegantly on the swell, and Françoise Hardy sang in the background "*Tous les garçons et les filles.*" I lit a cigarette and felt as if I was in a film. The air fizzed. I remember telling all this to Annie once, and Ellis couldn't remember a bloody thing. He's so disappointing at times. Couldn't remember the fishing boats, or Françoise Hardy, or how warm the evening was, and how the air fizzed—

Fizzed? he said.

Yes, I said. *Fizzed* with possibility or maybe excitement. I said to him that just because you can't remember doesn't mean the past isn't out there. All those precious moments are still there somewhere.

I think he's embarrassed by the word precious, said Annie.

Maybe, I said, looking at him.

. . .

I POUR OUT more wine and stand up. Look out across the cityscape and think London is so pretty. Music rises from a car below, its windows are down. David Bowie, "Starman." The car drives off and the night fades to silence.

BACK AT THE HOSPITAL in G's room. I hold his hand and I whisper to him, Cadmium Orange, Cerulean Blue, Cobalt Violet. He stirs. I stroke his head. Oxide of Chromium, Naples Yellow Light. This is my lullaby of color to him. I sense someone standing in the doorway and I turn round.

You're up, I say. I'm happy to see you.

Is this G? asks Chris.

You're not seeing him at his best, I'm afraid.

What were you saying to him? asks Chris.

Names of paint. He was an artist.

You're sweet, he says.

And you're looking good, I say.

I have a T-cell, he says.

Shut up, I say, or everyone'll want one.

He laughs. They think I'm doing better.

I can see you are.

I was angry with you.

I know.

But I miss talking with you.

I'm a dilemma, I say.

My friends have sent me a cake, he says. I feel like eating today.

Is this an invitation?

An olive branch, he says.

THE CAKE IS GOOD. Chocolate, not too sweet, and that awful word, moist. We eat half of it—me, most of it—and I feel bloated, and lie back in the chair and put my feet up on his bed. I'm embarrassed by my socks. Green terry toweling, the ones I wear when I clean the bathroom floor, fuck knows how they ended up in my good drawer.

Here, I say, hoping to distract him from looking at my socks. I hand him the photograph I was looking at three nights before.

This is me, I say. I'm nineteen. 1969.

He puts on his glasses and holds the photograph close.

You look so young, he says.

Ta, I say.

Who's that? he asks.

Ellis, I say.

Were you together?

I think so, I say. We were then.

Where was it taken?

In France, in the South.

You look cool.

We do, don't we?

Was he your first love?

Yes. Only one, probably.

Is he dead?

Oh God no. (Oh God no, not everyone dies, I want to say to him.)

Where's he now?

In Oxford. He has a wife. Annie.

Do you still see him?

No, I say.

He looks at me. Why?

Because . . . (And I realize I don't know how to answer this.) Because we lost contact. I lost contact.

You could get back in contact.

Yes. I could.

Don't you want him to know about this? Are you ashamed?

No! Not that, I say. No. It's complicated.

But it isn't, though, is it? Life isn't anymore, you told me that. All this makes life simple.

It's complicated, I say again. And there is an edge to my voice that stops him pursuing it.

He picks at my sock instead.

I know, I say. Awful.

Come on. Let's carry on with your letter, I say.

I don't want to write it today, he says. I want to know about this, and he waves the photograph in front of my face.

Oh blimey, I say, and I take my feet off the bed and I sigh and I stretch out my back.

And he says, You look like you're about to lift something heavy.

Ha! That is telling, I say.

FROM THE MOMENT I saw him, I wanted to kiss him. That's my well-practiced and preferred introduction to a conversation about Ellis. I used to wonder if my desire for him came out of displacement. My need to join with someone, my readiness to love. The consequence of grieving, even for a father who was, by then, as distant to me as the southern sky.

I have an image of Ellis and me in Oxford, standing at the window in my bedroom. It is night. The summer air is clammy, our chests are bare and we're wearing only our pajama bottoms. Our age? Fifteen, maybe. The window is open and we look out across the overgrown churchyard, and darkness has its own smell back then, and the smell is fecund and shitty, grassy and exciting, and we're listening out for the sounds of sex that rise from the crosses because that's where the drunks go for a moment of tenderness.

I'm nervous. And I can't look at him. And I reach down into his pants and hold him. I'm terrified he'll push me away but he doesn't. He moves me into the shadows and lets me wank him off. Afterward he's shy and thanks me and asks me if I'm all right. Never better, I say, and we laugh.

That was the start of our private world. A place where we didn't discuss who we were or what we were, just experimented with the other's body, and for years that was enough.

Sometimes, I wondered if his attraction to me was because I was the only one around, a release, of sorts. But when we were eighteen, he suggested a double date. We took the girls to a film, snogged them, and got them onto a bus home. Afterward, he and I came back to my room and got naked as if it was the most normal ending to an evening, like a strong coffee or an After Eight mint. Did I know I was gay? Yes, by then. But such compartmentalizing was irrelevant. We had each other and neither wanted more.

We got to France in August 1969 by sheer chance. A journalist I worked with at the *Oxford Times* went down to a villa there every year, and two months before he was due to go he had to cancel. He'd hardly finished telling me the story, when I said, I'll go! I'll take the room, and he was so amused by my enthusiasm, he made phone calls to France that very day to confirm the booking, and told me everything I needed to know about getting the train.

I raced to the Car Plant and met Ellis after shift. What's happened? he said. We're going to France, I said. What? he said. France, I said. France, France, and I started to poke him and he was all reserved, all—Stop it, not here, people are looking.

But the summer couldn't come fast enough. The weeks of waiting brought about a change between us, what I can only describe as a softening. The knowledge that what lay ahead was an opportunity for us to be different.

I remember standing on the ferry deck, as Dover receded. Our hands on the rail, my little finger touching his. The excitement of travel churning in my guts, an urge to kiss him, but of course, I couldn't. Suddenly, his finger moved against my skin. The electricity in my body could have lit up the fucking ship.

At Calais, we boarded *le train rapide* a little before eight. Just being the other side of the Channel, I remember, was so incredible. We'd never traveled for so long or so far. We left our compartment and joined others to smoke out in the crowded corridor, watching the changing shape of the country as we leaned out of windows, the air upon our faces fast and thrilling. As night fell, we bunked down in our cramped sleeper. Ellis sketched and I read. And I could hear his pencil moving across the page, and I felt so excited for him and for us, and every now and then a cheese baguette and a cup of red wine yo-yoed between us, and we felt so sophisticated, we really did. At Dijon, we were joined by a rude salesman who turned out the light without consulting us. So ending our first glorious night.

I remember dozing to the rhythm of the train. Listening to nocturnal sounds of railroad life as we carved through Lyon, Avignon, Toulon, before emerging into the Saint-Raphaël morning sun, where a taxi was waiting to take us into Agay and the Villa Roche Rose, our home for the next nine days. In the car we looked out and couldn't speak. Our mouths silenced by the intense color of the sky.

Our room was white and spacious, with two single beds that faced pale blue shutters, and the smell of a recently mopped terracotta floor, a strong hint of pine. I pulled back the shutters and sunlight streaked across the room. The red rock of the Massif de l'Esterel dominated the distance, window boxes of tuberose claimed the fore. We'd never seen anything more beautiful, I remember. And I thought of Dora in that moment, and I said, Your mum—

And he said, I know, as he always did. An instinctive closing of a door, too painful to open.

Our landlady, Madame Cournier, provided us with hand-drawn maps of the area, and we cycled straightaway into Saint-Raphaël to claim a modest space on a packed beach, our old gray towels embarrassed amidst the plethora of multicolored ones. We took up that position for days, and under a sheen of coconut oil our skin sizzled and browned, and we cooled off and healed in the weak drift of a Mediterranean tide.

I felt as if nothing else had previously existed. As if the colors and smells of this new country eradicated memory, as if every day rolled back to Day One, bringing with it the chance to experience it all again. I'd never felt more myself. Or more in tune to what I was and what I was capable of. A moment of authenticity when fate and blueprint collide and everything is not only possible, but within arm's reach. And I fell in love. Madly, intoxicatingly so. I think he may have, too. Just for a moment. But I never really knew.

We were in our bar down on the beach, drunk on a cocktail of pastis and Françoise Hardy, and it was late, and we could hear glasses being collected behind us.

Come on, he said, and we left the terrace and felt the cool of the sand on our bare feet. We continued along the beach away from our bikes, crept over the rocks at the far side of the bay, just as the road headed out toward Frejus Plage. It was sheltered and hidden from the voices that carried along the promenade above, and we chose to settle by a large rock, equidistant between the road and the sea. He looked about and began to quickly undress. It was so unlike him, I started to laugh. He kicked off his shorts and ran naked into the sea, white arse bobbing. He swam away from shore, rolled onto his back and floated. I stripped off hurriedly and followed him in. I swam toward him, dived under and pulled him down and kissed him. There was no struggle. We surfaced, laughing, and we turned toward each other and I felt his chest on mine. Felt his leg wrap around mine, and in that moment, away from home, I could see it in his eyes. Everything was different.

Suddenly, we were stumbling through the shallows, fell on top of one another in the damp sand. The intoxicating thrill of being drunk, of being naked, of being public surged through us. And, for a while, we didn't move because neither of us knew what the next move should be.

We crawled back into the shadow of the jutting rock, hands clasping one another's cocks, gorging on one another's mouths, until the proximity of the road above distracted us and made us nervous. Car lights flickered across the sand as traffic turned left, momentarily revealing our entwined legs and feet. We kept stopping to listen out for gendarmes who patrolled the beaches at night, and soon the fear of being caught overwhelmed us, and we hurriedly dressed, ran back along the beach to the Promenade where we'd left our bikes.

We didn't stop at the bakery, didn't buy the warm brioche that previously brought an end to our nights, we just kept on cycling, holding hands along deserted roadways, sometimes, dangerously close to the dark edge of the coast road. And sometimes, oncoming traffic suddenly appeared and swerved back into lane, unsuspecting that anyone else might be traveling in the opposite direction.

At the villa, we left our bikes at the side gate. He took out a key and we crept into the hallway. We avoided the middle stair, the creaking stair, and swiftly entered our room. The shutters were closed, and the air was still. Just us, alone, behaving like strangers. I was so nervous I could barely swallow. We were two people unsure what to do, relying solely on instinct.

I want to, I said. Me too, he said.

He locked the door. Made sure the keyhole was covered by the fall of a towel. We undressed separately, unbearably shy. I don't know what to do, he said. Me neither, I said. I lay down and opened my legs. I pulled him on top of me and told him he had to go slow.

THE SOUNDS of breakfast rose from downstairs.

Le café est prêt! shouted Madame Cournier.

I awoke hungry. I slipped out from under the sheet and walked to the window. I opened the shutters and the warm breeze wrapped around my body. I looked back at him sleeping. I wanted to wake him. I wanted him all over again.

I moved away from the window and pulled on a pair of swimming shorts. I knelt by the bed and thought, he'll wake up soon and he'll wonder what happened last night. And he'll wonder what it means he's become. And he'll feel shame and the creeping shadow of his father. I know this because I know him. But I won't let him.

He stirred. He opened his eyes. He sat up disorientated and scratched the salt in his hair. And there it was—all of a sudden—the reddening, the bewilderment, the withdrawing. But I caught it before it settled. Last night was amazing, I said. Amazing, amazing, amazing. And I kissed my way down his stomach—amazing—till he filled my mouth, and we smothered one another's coming till we could barely breathe.

The morning took us back along the coast road, past

Boulouris and the red dirt cliffs dotted with bougainvillea. He slowed and dropped behind. He got off his bike and left it at the side of the road. He walked out to the tip of the promontory, overlooking the bay. I cycled back to him and left my bike next to his. Fishing boats were out, the sea was still, the glare of the sun, white. We sat down on the ledge.

What is it? I said.

What if we don't go back home? he said.

You serious? I said.

What if we don't. Could we work?

Sure. We could pick grapes. Work in a hotel, a café maybe. People do. We could.

What about Mabel? he said.

Mabel would understand, I said.

I put my hand on his back and he didn't push it away.

You could paint and I could write, I said.

He looked at me. How incredible would that be? I said. Right, Ell?

And for the four remaining days—the ninety-six remaining hours—we mapped out a future away from everything we knew. When the walls of the map were breached, we gave one another courage to build them again. And we imagined our home an old stone barn filled with junk and wine and paintings, surrounded by fields of wildflowers and bees.

I remember our final day in the villa. We were supposed to be going that evening, taking the sleeper back to England. I was on edge, a mix of nerves and excitement, looking out to see if he made the slightest move toward leaving, but he didn't. Toiletries remained on the bathroom shelves, clothes stayed scattered across the floor. We went to the beach as usual, lay side by side in our usual spot. The heat was intense and we said little, certainly nothing of our plans to move up to Provence, to the lavender and light. To the fields of sunflowers.

I looked at my watch. We were almost there. It was happening. I kept saying to myself, he's going to do it. I left him on the bed dozing, and went out to the shop to get water and peaches. I walked the streets as if they were my new home. *Bonjour* to everyone, me walking barefoot, oh so confident, free. And I imagined how we'd go out later to eat, and we'd celebrate at our bar. And I'd phone Mabel and Mabel would say, I understand.

I raced back to the villa, ran up the stairs and died.

Our rucksacks were open on the bed, our shoes already packed away inside. I watched him from the door. He was silent, his eyes red. He folded his clothes meticulously, dirty washing in separate bags. I wanted to howl. I wanted to put my arms around him, hold him there until the train had left the station.

I've got peaches and water for the journey, I said.

Thank you, he said. You think of everything.

Because I love you, I said.

He didn't look at me. The change was happening too quickly.

Is there a taxi coming? My voice was weak, breaking.

Madame Cournier's taking us.

I went to the open window, the scent of tuberose strong. I lit a cigarette and looked at the sky. An airplane cast out a vivid orange wake that ripped across the violet wash. And I remember thinking, how cruel it was that our plans were out there somewhere. Another version of our future, out there somewhere, in perpetual orbit.

The bottle of pastis? he said.

I smiled at him. You take it, I said.

We lay in our bunks as the sleeper rattled north and retraced the journey of ten days before. The cabin was dark, an occasional light from the corridor bled under the door. The room was hot and airless, smelled of sweat. In the darkness, he dropped his hand down to me and waited. I couldn't help myself, I reached up and held it. Noticed my fingertips were numb. We'll be OK, I remember thinking. Whatever we are, we'll be OK.

We didn't see each other for a while back in Oxford. We both suffered, I know we did, but differently. And sometimes, when the day loomed gray, I'd sit at my desk and remember the heat of that summer. I'd remember the smells of tuberose that were carried by the wind, and the smell of octopus cooking on stinking griddles. I'd remember the sound of our laughter and the sound of a doughnut seller, and I'd remember the red canvas shoes I lost in the sea, and the taste of pastis and the taste of his skin, and a sky so blue it would defy anything else to be blue again. And I'd remember my love for a man that almost made everything possible.

A weekend toward the end of September, the bell above the door rang and there he was in the shop. Same old feeling in my guts.

I'll go if you want me to, he said.

I smiled, I was so fucking happy to see him.

You've only just got here, you twat, I said. Now give us a hand with this, and he took the other end of the trestle table and moved it over to the wall. Pub? I said.

He grinned. And before I could say anything else he put his arms around me. And everything he couldn't say in our room in France was said in that moment. I know, I said. I know. I'd already accepted I wasn't the key to unlock him. She'd come later.

It took a while to acknowledge the repercussions of that

time. How the numbness in my fingertips traveled to my heart and I never even knew it.

I had crushes, I had lovers, I had orgasms. My trilogy of desire, I liked to call it, but I'd no great love after him, not really. Love and sex became separated by a wide river and one the ferryman refused to cross. The psychiatrist liked that analogy. I watched him write it down. Chuckle, chuckle, his pen across the page.

So that was it, I say to Chris, when I get to the end of the story. Nine days and they never let me go.

And you never got back together afterward? he says.

No. We had our time. Friends only.

He looks thoughtful. He looks sad.

D'you need to sleep? I say.

Maybe.

I'm going to go then. I stand up.

Can I keep this tonight? he says, holding up the photo.

I'm surprised by what he asks. If you want, I say.

I'll give it back tomorrow. I will see you tomorrow, won't I?

I put on my shoes. Yes, I say, but tomorrow's a letter-writing day.

I get to the door and he calls my name. I turn.

He says, I wouldn't have packed. I would've let the train go.

I nod.

THE NEXT DAY, a burst of winter sun has made everybody bold. Chris has persuaded me to take him outside in a wheelchair and I've piled onto him as many regulation blankets as possible and forced a thick woolen hat onto his head. Don't be long, the young nurse Chloe says to me quietly. I won't, I mouth to her.

We sit by the fountain as sunlight dances white across the ripples and he closes his eyes as he faces the brittle warmth and dictates the final words of his letter. It is a beautiful letter, and his parents will receive it the following day and their world will be shattered. He's quiet because he knows this.

We could be anywhere, he says.

We could, I say.

Italy. Rome. What's the fountain there?

The Trevi? I say.

Have you seen it?

Yes, I have.

What's it like?

Underwhelming, I say.

He looks at me.

A bit fussy, I say.

You're doing it to me again, he says.

I'm not. Seriously. It's just an opinion. It's not like here, I say.

Idiot, he says.

I grin.

D'you think throwing money into any fountain is lucky? he says.

I do, actually. I'm a fountain expert, I say, and I give him a coin from my pocket.

I wheel him close to the edge of the water. He blinks as spray catches his face. Minuscule rainbows darting like midges. The coin sinks. His mouth moves, a silent incantation of hope.

Take me out of here, he says.

Out of the chair? I say.

No. The gates, he says. Out of here.

I look at my watch. I look at him. I wheel him toward the entrance and stop at the border.

Do we dare? I say teasingly. Do we dare? A little nudge across the threshold.

We dare! he says, and I wheel him out into a city on the move.

Over there, he says, and I stop at a bench near the gates.

I sit down next to him, sunshine on our faces. We could be anywhere, he says again. His pale arm fights free of the blankets and reaches for my hand. He closes his eyes. Rome, he says.

IT'S THREE in the morning and I'm awake. I feel like I'm coming down with something. My mind whirrs and my pulse is all over the place. Sometimes my heart fails to beat, and I lie in an airless limbo. I'm scared. I don't want to go through all this, I don't want my body to fail. I only acknowledge this when I'm alone. I pick up the phone. Maybe I could call them but I don't know what to say. Maybe Annie would answer and that would be easier.

Annie, it's me, I'd say (in a slightly pathetic whisper).

Mikey? she'd say.

I'm sorry it's late, I'd say (being respectful, polite).

Where are you?

London, I'd say.

Are you OK? she'd say.

Yeah, really good, I'd say (lying).

We miss you, she'd say.

I replace the phone quietly and stare at the ceiling. I try the conversation again.

Annie, it's me, I'd say.

You sound awful, she'd say. Are you OK?

No. I start crying.

A STINKING COLD has kept me away from the hospital the last four days. Sneezing. Runny nose, irritated eyes. It disappears after four days, and I declare myself well. I've never been so grateful for a mere cold.

I decide not to go to the ward till later that afternoon and go instead to the West End to see a film that everyone has been talking about. I sit in the front row of an almost empty cinema where seventy-two frames of color flicker across my face every second, and where a young man stands on a desk in the final moments and cries out in love, O Captain, my Captain!

And there I am, thirteen again, at Long Bridges bathing place, reciting a poem I thought I'd long forgotten. Word after word of Whitman's poem tumbles out, as sunlight plays on the surface of the Thames.

It's a poem about grief, I say to Dora.

> O Captain! my Captain! rise up and hear the
>   bells;
> Rise up—for you the flag is flung—for you the
>   bugle trills;

For you bouquets and ribbon'd wreaths—for you
   the shores a-crowding;
For you they call, the swaying mass, their eager
   faces turning . . .

Dora bends down and kisses me on the head. She walks
to the water's edge and I race after her. Pretend to save me
from drowning, I say and I jump in the river and swim to
the middle of the pond, arms and legs kicking and flailing.
She swims toward me, whispers to me to lean back, to let
go. Everything's going to be all right, Michael, she says, as
she pulls me across those warm, still waters. And all the
way, I quote,

   O Captain! my Captain!

I race back to the hospital because I want to tell Chris
about the film. And I've played it in my head, so many
times, what I'm going to say to him when I get back to the
ward. I'm going to stand in the doorway and recite the
poem from start to finish. It will be like theater. The doorway the stage, he the audience, and the nurses may stop to
listen. I know already how it will be. Something good in a
difficult day. When I arrive at Chris's room, my knees fail.
The bed has been stripped, and the room is empty. Chloe

sees me. She rushes over. It's OK, Michael, she says. It's OK. His parents came. They've taken him home.

I'M IN G'S ROOM watching the late news. The BBC reporting from Germany. The Berlin Wall is down and the gates are open. Cars are honking, friends and families are reunited and champagne is drunk. Chloe comes in and brings me a tea. She puts her arm around me and says, nodding to the TV, No one thought this was possible ten years ago. And now look. Life changes in ways we can never imagine. Walls come down and people are free. You wait, she says.

I know what she's trying to say: Hope.

G died on 1 December 1989. I haven't cried. But sometimes I feel as if my veins are leaking, as if my body is overwhelmed, as if I'm drowning from the inside.

I'VE TAKEN TO THE SOFA. I'm not sure of the date, I don't care. I feel so heavy, I can barely move. I eat vegetable broth, and lots of it. I'm aware, some days, how this flat must smell.

Every time I stand up, I rearrange the cushions on this sofa so it's ready for me to lie back down again. Small gestures are important. I lie facing the balcony, and in the evenings, I lose myself in the transfer of light. Sometimes I open the sliding doors and hear Christmas approach. I hear the chatter of who's going where and who's buying what. I listen to the drunken songs from office party revelers and sometimes I make it outside and watch illicit snogging in the shadows. I wonder if this stolen act is the start of something or the end of something.

THE DIGITAL CLOCK flicks over. At 18:03, there's a knock at my door. I look through the peephole. I see a woman's face—a kind face, sort of familiar, but not a friend. I open the door and she says, Michael? (I'm surprised she knows my name.) She says, I'm Lee. Maybe you don't remember me? Four doors down that way, she says, pointing.

She says, I haven't seen you out the last few days and I thought you could do with a few things. I tried you yesterday, but . . .

And she hands me a large bag of shopping.

There's wine, too, she says. So careful when you put it down.

I stare at her. I say, Thank you, and begin to unravel.

I feel her hand on my shoulder.

She says, You know, if you need anything over Christmas, we're staying put and—

I cut her off before her kindness overtakes me. I thank her again, and wish her a happy time.

I empty the bag on the kitchen counter. Potatoes, wine, a ham and a pork pie and salad, a feast. Chocolate, too. A card. On the front, an image of Victorian London under snow. Inside, With Our Very Best Wishes, Lee and Alan.

I put the card on the table and it makes a difference to the room, to my mood especially. It's *Christmassy*. I light a candle and open the sliding doors. Traffic and chill air. Lee and Alan. Who knew?

CHRISTMAS 1976. The sudden fall of light along Cowley Road. The smell of chestnuts Mabel roasts in the kitchen and sells in the shop. The smell of oranges punctured by cloves. The holly sprigs and mistletoe that Ellis and I used to gather out at Nuneham Courtenay.

I say to Ellis, Last tree and we're done.

Where to? he says.

Divinity Road, I say. Up by Hill Top. Here's the invoice, and I hand him the sheet.

He looks at it. Anne Cleaver, he says.

See you afterward—

——Course, he says.

Eat here?

Great, he smiles. He leaves the shop, tree on his shoulder, fur hat on his head, and I watch him cross the road. I sit down in Mabel's armchair. The clock ticks over, and customers come in and make additions to their orders. But mostly, I read. Truman Capote, *Breakfast at Tiffany's*, *A Christmas Memory*. I go out the back to make a cup of tea. I look at the clock and wonder where he's got to.

In seven years, France has changed in our storytelling. It is now a holiday of single beds and single lads, sunbathing and French beauties. We keep secrets from one another now, secrets about sexual adventures, who's done what. They're secret because we don't know what to do about the thing we were. So we stay away from it and don't touch it, in case it stings. Avoidance is the dock leaf.

He's taking forever. I'm hungry. Mabel's not back from her friend's, and I feel like company. The cold inches across the stone floor and finds my toes. I stand up. I jump about. I go over to the record player and search out my favorite record. The introduction plays and my heart shimmies. The Impressions. "People Get Ready." I open the shop door and let my feet take me across the floor.

I sing, I close my eyes. I look up. In the doorway, Sister Teresa is laughing. Ho, ho, ho, I say. I offer her my hand,

and surprisingly, she accepts. We slow waltz at arm's length, and between us is the faint smell of soap and incense. I've known her for many years and let my thirteen-year-old self serenade her with his confusion and chafing hormones. We separate and she returns to the doorway. I finger-click my way to the back curtain and when I turn round, I miss a beat. Ellis is standing there with a young woman by his side, her red-blond hair vivid against the shoulders of her navy duffel coat. There is a familiarity to them already, no space between their bodies, and I know they've already kissed. She's smiling at me and she has eyes that question, and I know I'll have trouble with those eyes, one day. I don't want the music to end. I want to keep singing and dancing because I need time to know what to say because I know she's the One, and I just need time.

I WAKE WITH A JOLT. As if the car I'm in has crossed a cattle-grid. It's a New Decade, I know it is. The nineties. How incredible. I roll over and stay put for days.

THE CLOCKS HAVE gone forward and mornings are light. I go into Soho to do something enjoyable because I feel so fucking normal, it hurts. I'm out of the worst of it, I know I am. All I needed was time.

I sit outside Bar Italia huddled under a blue sky. I begin to read a newspaper but I can't be bothered. I see faces I know and we smile and nod. I order a macchiato. I send it back because it's not quite how I like it, but they know me and know how I am, I've been a regular for years. Inside, Sinatra sings "Fly Me to the Moon": Annie's song. It was legendary how badly she used to sing it.

Every time Annie sings an angel loses its wings. That's what I used to say.

Be nice, Mikey, she'd say, stroking my face. Be nice.

I walk down Charing Cross Road and notice black blotches of chewing gum on the pavements. Why do people do that? Why don't they care? I feel the effects of the coffee in my chest and back, a growing tightness.

I climb the steps to the National Gallery and feel dizzy. I sit by the bookshop and think of G. He's distant. I feel nothing. He's gone. I walk through the rooms, annoyed by the presence of others.

I stand in front of a painting of fifteen sunflowers, and I think of too many things and I start to hurt and the pain is intense. What did you see, Dora? Tell me what you saw.

I turn sharply. The man next to me is saying, Can you move?

I ignore him. I feel him pushing me. I turn. *What?* I say. A photo? Wait, I say.

Pushing me, pushing me, pushing me.

Don't fucking push me! someone screams. I have a right to be here! Got it? *I have a fucking right to be here.* A fucking right.

And I'm frozen because the words are mine, and I don't know what to do because everyone's looking at me, and now the security man's coming toward me and I need to make people not feel frightened of me, because I'm not a frightening person. And I raise my hands and say, I'm going. It's OK, I'm going. And I back out and people are staring at me, and I'm apologizing. I feel dizzy but I mustn't collapse, I have to make it to the door. I'm sorry, I keep muttering. Out into the cold now. Keep walking, I'm so sorry, keep walking.

June 1990, France

'm here, Dora, I've come south. Stone cottages, fields of lavender and olive groves. Van Gogh's dark cypresses spear the sky. I'm here for you, Dora Judd. Do you remember when I was twelve and, one day, you said to me, Call me Dora. Do you remember? And I said, Dora? Such a pretty name, Mrs. Judd. And you laughed and said, You're like an old man sometimes, Michael. And I said, Do you think you were named after Dora Maar? And Ellis said, Who's Dora Maar? And you said, Picasso's muse. And Ellis said, What's a muse? And you said, A rare force, personified as a woman, who inspires creative artists. Just like that, you said it. As if you'd memorized it. I remember it word for word. No pause. No thought. Personified as a woman. That's what you said. Why I remember all this now, I don't know. Why am I scribbling to you, my dear dead long-gone friend, I do not know. Maybe, at least, to say you are my muse, Dora. I'm here because of you. Because of the night you won a painting in a raffle.

Lilacs are scattered around the scrubby land, and the chalky blue hills of the Alpilles rise beyond. I'm so tired now, I've walked for days. Humidity confuses my thoughts. My clothes are drenched and the sweating frightens me and an overwhelming need to shit propels me off the path. I ditch my rucksack and crouch behind a bush and just about manage to scratch away at the earth and squat a hole before I explode. The clouds are low and gray, acting as a thick blanket keeping the heat in, so stifling so still. A low rumble of thunder shakes the sky toward the Alpilles. But there'll be no rain, there'll be no surrender. Ah, the simple joy of finding a tissue in one's pocket, it's those little things. I pull up my trousers and cover the hole. Thunder rumbles again. No rain, but around me the ants are out in droves. I feel empty, finally, and wonder why that's a good feeling.

I drink water and it's warm. It leaves my thirst unquenched. I can veer off this track anytime I want to. I come across signposts to towns and hotels and could easily divert and seek comfort, but I don't. I'm forcing myself into this solitude and keep on walking. There's something about movement—the necessity of movement to deal with trauma. Academic papers have been written about it and I've read them. How animals shake to release fear in their muscles. I do that too. Under the sun amidst the scrub, I shake, I shout, I scream. So I keep to the track, transfixed by the motion of walking, trusting in an invisible remedy that will make me feel human once again.

The sound of bleating makes me look up, and I see a small abandoned monastery ahead. I think it's abandoned, as part of it is clearly in ruin and has become shade for a small herd of white goats. But as I get closer, I see that the building is, in fact, a home of sorts. I drop my rucksack and sit down on the smooth front steps that have already absorbed the heat of the day. I unlace my boots and take off my socks, and know immediately, I won't be traveling any farther that afternoon. I'll share shelter and shade with goats and will fall asleep to the music of their language.

I doze. For how long, I'm not sure. The heat hasn't lessened at all. I'm aware of company, though, and thought it may have been an inquisitive goat seeking me out. But I open my eyes and see a priest. A little older than me, maybe, it's hard to tell. But he has a kind face, benevolent eyes, and the dark skin of the South. He's carrying a large terracotta bowl of water, and floating lavender heads release a subtle scent. He places the bowl next to me and goes back inside. I put my feet in the bowl and the sensation's heavenly. He comes back out and I notice a quiver of a smile on his lips. I suddenly realize the water is for my hands and face.

The room I'm taken to is dark and still. The slight smell of damp stone remains, frankincense too. I move the shutter away from the window and look out onto rows of purple lavender. The sound of bees and cicadas is the faint musical backdrop to this scene, the goats, too, and their bells. I turn around but the priest has gone. My rucksack has been placed next to a small iron-framed bed and above the bed is a crucifix. Next to the bed a desk and on the desk an altar candle. I lift the crucifix off the wall and put it on the desk and cover it with my shirt. I hear footsteps climbing the stairs. I open the door slightly and catch a glimpse of two backpackers heading toward the room above. I can't see if they're men or women. The packs are big.

Night falls and, with it, my anxiety. I watch the shift of light through the window, the orange lights from farms in the distance. When the sky reaches the blackest navy, stars appear, mostly white but sometimes I see pink. Above me, the sound of a body falling onto a bed. A sliver of light seeps beneath my door. A shadow across the floor, the low rumble of thunder. A knock at the door brings me to my feet.

Light floods in. The priest carries a tray of bread and fruit and cheese and an opened bottle of wine. He places the tray on the desk, lights the candle and turns to go.

I reach out for his arm. Eat with me. Please. There's enough, I say.

The priest stays. We eat. We don't speak, but we drink from the same glass. The long walk has reinstated my appetite and my mouth comes alive to the sourness of the bread, the musty ooze of the cheese, the succulent sweetness of the apricots. Thank you, I say. *Merci*. My head shaking slightly, in disbelief and in gratitude.

Forks of lightning touch low across the horizon but still no rain. The bats have claimed the sky from the swallows and the smell of lavender and sweetness rises from the earth. I stand at the window. Occasionally, the scent of honey from the candle falls on my nose.

I sense the shifting sound of movement behind me. Was that breath? The feel of a body up close against me. I don't move because I have nothing to offer anyone anymore. I sense buttons being unfastened and fabric peeling away from skin.

I turn round. The priest is nowhere near me and I feel ashamed by my mistaken desire. The room cools sharply as the first of the rain falls. The priest comes toward me now, and he holds me by the shoulders. His eyes are gentle, his eyes are wounded. It's as if he knows. I hold on to his arms and let my head fall. I'm broken by my need for others. By the erotic dance of memory that pounces when loneliness falls.

I awake early to the sound of a bell ringing. I walk

across to the window and look out onto the landscape. The backpackers are on their way, and the goats continue to feast, unconcerned, in the scrub. I hobble over to the dinner tray and eat some bread and cheese. I pour out the last of the wine before I shower.

I leave money on the table and replace the crucifix on the wall. There are to be no good-byes, just an open door leading to sunshine. The overnight rain, I find, has released the scent of a benevolent earth. I'm grateful to his God and care.

THE CHAÎNE DES ALPILLES at the southern edge of Saint-Rémy are strung out blue in the early light, and mist rises from these hills. I begin my walk. Roads and scrubland and farmland. Olive trees scattered along the way, their gray-green leaves catching every ripple of June's seductive breath.

I sit on a stone and face the ascent of the sun and revel in the light of the South. The cicadas are loud and their song unrelenting.

I remember telling G the story of the cicada song and he was as unimpressed as ever by the arbitrary knowledge that used to escape my lips. I said that ancient Greeks were so besotted by these little fellas that they used to keep them

in cages so they could fawn over them and listen to them
whenever they wanted. G said he thought they did that to
young men, too. You have a point, I said. But . . .

And I continued.

I said, They live underground for most of their lives in
a kind of larval stage, drinking sap from roots. Then, after
about three years, they emerge into the heat of midsum-
mer, climb out onto a nearby plant and shed their skin.
That's when the transformation begins, I said. And it's
only during the last three weeks of their lives that they live
above ground and the males call out their song. And sometimes it's for mating and sometimes protest. So what d'you
think? I said.

Think about what? he said.

The story. It sounds familiar, right?

Oh God, he said. This isn't an analogy for gay men, is it?

Think about it, I said. We all had to come out of the
dark to sing.

BY MIDDAY, the heat is unforgiving and the road has
turned to dust, a white dust that coats my boots and shins.
The Judas trees are in bloom, and large black bees are
noisy in their work, their bodies heavy with pollen.

I come to a *mas* with rooms, and I like the look of it. Far enough away from town but not too far should I ever have the need. The vacant sign is so discreet, it's almost an afterthought in its appeal for guests.

I'm shown a quiet first-floor room that overlooks the grounds at the back. The sharp smell of grouting in the bathroom highlights a recent renovation. I lay out my few toiletries on the shelf above the basin. I unpack my rucksack and hang my clothes in front of the window, hoping the summer breeze will remove the faint smell of damp canvas they've absorbed from an old pair of trainers I should have thrown out long ago.

The late afternoon sun is still hot, and I strip off and leave my pants and T-shirt in the sink, where I'll wash them later with shampoo.

And now, I'm nervous. Naked in front of the mirror, I scour every inch of my body, searching for those telltale purple smudges that have afflicted others. I find nothing. The odd mosquito bite, of course, by my ankles and at the back of my knees. I sit on the bed and my fear is subsumed by the yellow warmth and comfortable surroundings. I breathe deeply and slowly, and I let the moment pass.

I put on my swimming shorts and go down the stairs, out across the gardens toward the shimmering absinthe-color pool.

I'm thankful poolside is quiet. People are sleeping off

lunches or out in their cars following the wine trails of Les Baux-de-Provence. I lay out my towel on a lounger, shaded by a windbreak of oleander. A sweet catch of music rears beyond a hedge, a forgotten radio turned low so as not to disturb. When the breeze ripples, petals of pink and white and fuchsia fall on me and I imagine myself a garlanded pyre alight under the fiery sun.

ANNIE ONCE ASKED ME what Ellis and I talked about. I said, Nothing really, because it was true, but she didn't seem convinced. And she laughed the way she always did, a response to her incredulity. Oh, Mikey, she said, and she grabbed my face and kissed my forehead. You beautiful sweet scamp, she said.

It was 1977 and she and I were new friends. We were getting drunk in a restaurant in Soho, an old-guard Italian one in Dean Street. We'd just bought her wedding dress at a secondhand shop in Covent Garden, lured in by a Gallic-themed window display, all Capri pants and Breton shirts and trilbies. *Breathless* to a T.

When she came out of the changing room wearing the dress that would take her down the aisle, I whistled loudly. She frowned and said, You've never done that before. And I said, I've never had the need.

I bought the dress for her while she was changing back into her favorite jeans.

I lifted the bottle, poured out more wine and continued the conversation. I said that Ellis and I talked of things in the moment. I said we just existed in each other's presence, because that's how it felt. Often in silence. And to a child it was a good silence, because nothing felt misconstrued. There was a safety to our friendship, I said. We just fit, I remember saying.

She became quiet and thoughtful. She told me that she'd once asked Ellis if we'd ever kissed. She said he looked at her, trying to fathom out what she wanted him to say. After a while, he said, We might have once, but we were young.

She told me she thought it quite a trite answer because she always knew it was more than that, more than youth. She just wanted to know, she said, to be part of us. There's something about first love, isn't there? she said. It's untouchable to those who played no part in it. But it's the measure of all that follows, she said.

I couldn't look at her.

She got up and went to the bathroom. I paid the bill and the waiters cleared the table. I was ready to go back to our shitty B&B in Bloomsbury, when I saw her heading toward me, face flushed and eyes bright.

Let's go out, she said. I wanna go where you go, she said.

She gripped my arm and we walked along neon-stained sidewalks through to Charing Cross Road and the Astoria. We waited outside while I lit us a cigarette and scanned the flavors of men going in. Her eyes were on me, I could feel her watching. Shovels uncovering my years of hiding. I smiled. Blew out smoke. I flicked my cigarette into the gutter. Come on, I said.

The sound of Thelma Houston pulsed through our hands as we paid our entry, and we were swept along in a fug of aftershave and sweat, into a group of bare-chested clones singing "Don't Leave Me This Way." Oh my fucking God! shouted Annie.

Look! The stage was heaving with gyrating bodies. Leather queens in a dance-off with punks, and among them, suburban kids living a long-contested fantasy.

I handed Annie a beer. The music was too loud for conversation so we drank fast and a change of record propelled us back onto the floor. "Dance Little Lady Dance." And oh we did! The light show flared off satin shorts and glistening shoulders and I felt overdressed and I took off my T-shirt, Annie laughing at me. I can't hear you, I shouted. Her hand on her chest. I. Love. This. And on the large screen behind her, Busby Berkeley dance routines played on a loop.

The air was flecked with sweat and stank of poppers, and leather boys danced hard. The light show dared itself, and strobes caught the delight on Annie's face, her hair plastered to her forehead. A mustachioed man danced next to us, white vest and gloves. He stuck a small bottle under her nose and I watched her gasp. You OK? I mouthed. She nodded, stunned. Fuck, she mouthed. Smiled.

Black light drenched the room and her teeth glowed brilliant white. Her bra too, visible at the deep V of her shirt. I pointed. The gloved hands were raised above us, fingers flickering like feathers. Look, Annie! Doves flying! I shouted. I gasp. A hand down the back of my jeans has found my crack. A blast of poppers hits my nose and my heart thumps to the bass notes of desire.

In the silence, in the dark, the shitty B&B didn't seem so bad. It was two a.m. and our ears were ringing. I had a slight headache encroaching and I knew she must have too. Oh forgive me, nose and brain. I was restless and much too hot. I drank chlorinated tap water out of a plastic cup and almost choked on my thirst.

You don't have to sleep on the sofa, said Annie, from the double bed she'd booked as two singles. I'm fine, I said. Really.

She sat up. Her body a silhouette backlit by streetlamps.

Mikey, she said. If you ever met anyone—

I know, I said.

I didn't want this conversation and I cut her off before it broke ground. The idea was incompatible. I could never bring anyone into our three. I had no room to love anyone else.

OUT BEYOND THE CONFINES of the *mas*, dusk envelops the land. Evening light falls upon the walls and dusts them in pink, and dark shadows press upon these walls. I'm aware of my loneliness in the intermittent silence along the road. An occasional car up ahead turns onto gravel. The shrill pipe of swallows above me, annoying then reassuring, dark arrowheads across the sky, their last dance with sun. I walk as far as the olive groves, but not as far as town. I want company, I don't want company. I turn back. My fickleness knows I'm too agitated to sleep.

The candles are extinguished on the dining tables and the outside gates locked, and quiet chatter snubbed by sleep. I go up to my room and change. I rub mosquito cream over my body and put on my swimming shorts and T-shirt. I walk downstairs, out across the grass, along the stony track toward the azure light of the pool.

The sunloungers have been repositioned and their cushions put away till the morning. I pull off my T-shirt. I crouch down and feel the temperature of the water. It feels cold after the heat of the day. I don't dive in, but jump. I bend my legs and the bottom of the pool swiftly meets my feet. I surface and begin to swim. My arms blade through the water. One, two, three, I turn to the left and breathe. At the wall, in deep water, I flip. Disorientation and bubbles, a brief moment of letting go, but all too brief, and my feet push against the concrete side, and my arms blade, and I breathe, and my anger propels me, back and forth until my lungs burn and my head feels tight and there are no thoughts just a body in motion. And every length I swim, I slough off a layer of hospital visits, of smells, of hopelessness, of medication, of young men who became old too fast, and I swim and I swim and I swim.

In the middle of the pool, I stop. Facedown, floating not breathing. I used to do it all the time as a kid out at Long Bridges. Learned to float before I could swim. Ellis never believed it was called dead man's float, thought I'd made it up. I told him it was a survival position after a long, exhausting journey. How apt.

All I see below is blue light. Peaceful and eternal. I'm holding my breath until my body throbs as one pulse. I roll over and suck in a deep lungful of warm air. I look up at the starry starry night. The sound of water in and out of my ears, and beyond this human shell, the sound of cicadas fills the night.

I dreamed of my mother. It was an image, that's all, and a fleeting one, at that. She was faded with age, like a discarded offcut on the studio floor. In this dream, she didn't speak, just stepped out of the shadows, a reminder that we are the same, her and me, cut from the same bruised cloth. I understand how she got up one day and left, how instinctively she trusted the compulsion to flee. The rightness of that action. We are the same, her and me.

She walked out when I was eight. Never came back. I remember being collected from school by our neighbor Mrs. Deakin, who bought me sweets on the way home and let me play with a dog for as long as I wanted. Inside the house, my father was sitting at the table, drinking. He was holding a sheet of blue writing paper covered in black words, and he said, Your mother's gone. She said she's sorry.

A sheet of writing paper covered in words and just two for me. How was that possible?

Her remnant life was put in bags and stored in the spare room at the earliest opportunity. Stuffed in, not folded— clothes brushes, cosmetics all thrown in together, awaiting collection from the Church. My mother had taken only what she could carry.

One rainy afternoon, when my father had gone next door to fix a pipe, I emptied the bags onto the floor and saw my mother in every jumper and blouse and skirt I held up. I used to watch her dress and she let me. Sometimes, she asked my opinion about colors or what suited her more, this blouse or that blouse? And she'd follow my advice and tell me how right I was.

I took off my clothes and put on a skirt first, then a blouse, a cardigan, and slowly I became her in miniature. She'd taken her good shoes, so I slipped on a pair of mid-height heels many sizes too big, of course, and placed a handbag on my arm. I stood in front of the mirror, and saw the infinite possibilities of play. I strutted, I pouted, the satin lining of the skirt clinging to my skin, electrifying the fine hairs on my legs.

What the fuck d'you think you're doing? said my father.

I hadn't heard him come in. He repeated the question.

Playing, I said.

Get that stuff off and go to your room.

I began to undress, burning with shame and humiliation.

And the skirt, said my father.

The skirt slid to the floor, exposing my nakedness. My father looked away in disgust.

I want to keep this, I said, holding up the handbag.

No.

Just to put my pencils in.

If you ever take it out of this fucking house—

I waited for the conclusion of this threat but it never came. My father disappeared downstairs and out of the front door, leaving me naked, bewildered, orphaned before time. I was too young, too confused to understand fully what happened in that room. That my father had said so little had been the wound, though. For him there was nothing to discuss because discussion would have made the moment real, just as my mother's departure had been so real. Instead, I was swept under the carpet to join her.

I see how decisions are made, in moments like that, that change the trajectory of one's life. Well, he won't like football, will he? He won't like sport, he won't like getting dirty. He won't like doing boy things.

So when my father went off to his football matches, I went to Mrs. Deakin's to read, or to make cakes with her for the church fayre. But I wanted to shout, I like football too! and I want to be with you. I want to be around men and their laughter and their ways! But in four years, I was never invited. And I retreated further into the background until I could barely be seen against the wallpaper and curtains, until I eventually disappeared, erased by the notion of what a boy with a handbag should be like.

I never did use the bag for pencils because it was too

precious. I put valuable things inside, instead. Marbles. French coins. A list of all the books I'd ever read. A pearl-handled penknife. And when I emptied out the bag, one day, caught on the penknife was a piece of thread, a different color to the lining. I pulled at the thread and it became loose, and I just kept pulling until a sliver of lining came away. And behind the lining was a small black-and-white photograph showing a woman walking toward the camera. She was quite pretty and wore sunglasses and she was smiling, her arm outstretched toward the person who was taking the picture, my mother, I presumed. I didn't know this woman but the picture was taken at Trafalgar Square because I recognized the lions and the gallery in the background.

As I grew older, I came to understand this woman was my mother's freedom. We love who we love, don't we? I hope she loved her.

IT'S A RARE overcast day and I walk over to Mausole, to the St. Paul asylum where van Gogh spent a year before he died. The air along this stretch of road is filled with the scent of honeysuckle that has crept over a neighboring wall. I think it's honeysuckle. It's sweet and fragrant, but I'm not good with plants—that was Annie's thing. I veer off through olive groves where the sun has yet to take the color out of the wildflowers. In two weeks, though, the grass will be scorched and lifeless.

The pines along the avenue drip with earlier rain. Daylight is flat and shy, and the air fecund, not stifling. Clouds are low and blanketing, and there is peace. In the chapel, my nose pricks with the fumes of decay and I quickly leave those moribund stones to their plangent tale. Outside, the world is vital. I take comfort in the ochre-colored building opposite, where the doves cry aloft.

Ahead of me two coaches pull up and scores of tourists disembark. I feel angry because I'm not ready for people. For over a week, I've kept to myself at the *mas*. Have eaten breakfast and dinner in the shadow of overhanging trees and have occupied the lone sunlounger at the far end of the pool. I'm just not ready.

The sky explodes with rain and a deep growl reverberates across the dark low clouds. I watch from under a pine tree as people scream and scramble for shelter. And then just like that, the clouds break and the sun appears and the air is seething, and leaves steam, and plastic macs are peeled off and cameras come out again. This is not how I planned the day. And instead of going back to the *mas*, I take off across the fields, and I climb away and climb high into the garrigue and rosemary. I look down, like a Roman ghost, on the ruins at Glanum. The footfall of the past whispers across the millennia. In the distance, I can see Saint-Rémy and the oscillation of Avignon. I can see the Alps. I venture further into the landscape. If it was a man I would call it rugged and thoughtful and scruffy. If it was a man I think it would be Ellis.

IT'S YOUR WEDDING DAY, Ell. You've stayed the night at the shop because it would be bad luck to see Annie's dress. You're standing at the window in my bedroom overlooking the churchyard. You turn and face me as I come up the stairs and I'm surprised to see you're not dressed yet. You've showered, and dried yourself badly. Your hair is wet and your back glistens and the top of your boxer shorts are damp. You say, D'you remember . . . ?

And you talk about the time you came here after Dora died, after your father forced you to punch the good out of your life. How you climbed the stairs to this room with bruised knuckles and swollen eyes, how I held the wrap of ice against your hand and told you that life would get better. And, I realize, the story's not about Dora, or your father, or grief. But about us.

D'you remember? you say at the end.

Yes.

Come on, Ell, I say. And you turn away from the window and come toward me. I hand you your watch. Your hands are shaking. I hold up your white shirt, still warm from the iron, and you slip your arms into the sleeves. You attempt the buttons, but your fingers are clumsy and thick.

I don't know what's wrong with me, you say.

Nerves, I say, and I button your shirt up myself. I hand you your trousers and you slip them on. You say, I think my boxers are wet. I say nothing. I've noticed your socks are inside out but I say nothing. I run the narrow tie around your collar and knot it. I fold your collar down, make small adjustments. Your breath smells of toothpaste. I gently pick off the scrap of toilet paper stuck to your chin. Not bleeding, I say. I thread plain silver cuff links through your cuffs and you tuck your shirt into your trousers, zip up.

Shoes? I say.

Scuffed brogues. You sit on the bed and put them on. The only thing I asked you to do.

You stand up. I hold your suit jacket and you put it on.

Hair, I say, and you run your hands through it, and it's almost dry.

Right, I say.

And I take a step back. The suit is of a decade before.

Lightweight navy wool, two buttons, narrow lapels and narrow trouser legs that stop at the top of the shoe. White shirt. Thin maroon tie with two navy stripes. I brush your shoulders with my hand.

Will I do? you say.

Very handsome, I say, matter-of-fact.

My words avoid the lump in my throat.

You've got the ring? you say.

I take it out of my pocket. Check, I say.

Mabel shouting, Car's here!

I offer you my hand.

You look at me. You say, Thank—

It's OK, I say. Come on, let's go.

NIGHTS ARE MY RECOVERY. The walk across the gardens as the *mas* sleeps. The ritual of undressing under a black night, the sensation of water as I jump in, as I rise and break surface. The power in my arms and legs drawing me along. One, two, three, breathe. I flip, I turn. My thoughts numbed by the monotony, my rage tamed by the rigor. And in the iridescent blue, I slowly meet myself again.

I sit long after dinner in the spray of candlelight, blessed by the smoke of mosquito coils, and I drink the local rosé as if it is water. I listen to other people's conversations because my understanding of French has improved. And an elderly couple, who have been there all week, pass by my table and say, *Bonsoir, monsieur*. And I raise my glass, and say *Bonsoir* back to them.

I stand at the edge of the pool and close my eyes. Not a breeze. Just my breath. And it's loud because my mouth is open and I'm breathing from the depth of my stomach, and tonight my stomach churns and I don't know why. I slip into the water and begin to swim. My pace is fierce as it always is but soon my breathing becomes ragged, a sudden explosion of in-breaths, and then I'm gasping. I have to stop swimming, I'm treading water, I'm going nowhere and I'm crying. Abandoned by the rage that fueled me, I'm consumed by an overwhelming sadness that's left me un-anchored in the middle of the pool. And there I cry for everyone. For Chris, for G, for my mother and father and Mabel, and for the nameless faces that fall away each year. And I struggle between my tears, and can do little else but make for the side.

I rest till I'm calm and my breathing has settled. I lift myself out and sit by the edge of the pool with a towel around my shoulders. And I wonder what the sound of a heart breaking might be. And I think it might be quiet, unperceptively so, and not dramatic at all. Like the sound of an exhausted swallow falling gently to earth.

.   .   .

THE THIRD WEEK of June is my time to leave the *mas*. New holidaymakers are moving into my room and I have to go. When I pay, the manager, Monsieur Crillon, says to me in English: Come back soon.

I walk along the stone track where rows of lavender and oleander challenge a hundred shades of green. At the end of the road, at the crossroads, I stop and wonder what I'm doing. I'm not ready to leave. I don't want to leave. Instead of waving down the bus, I turn back to where I've come from.

This is soon, says Monsieur Crillon, smiling. I'm looking for a job, I say in French.

The manager tells me there are no more jobs for men, and the only vacancy he has is for a chambermaid, that's all. A position made free that morning. Not for a man, he says, cleaning rooms. He shakes his head. Not for a man, he says.

I say, I can do that. I've done that, give me a week's trial.

He stares at me. He thinks it over. He shrugs. He gives me a week's trial.

I change the sheets and launder the sheets and clean the toilets and wipe down the showers and sweep the flagstones. And each job, to me, is proof that I still can care. And the little touches I leave in my wake, the small jars of lavender or vetiver or rosemary, or the carefully arranged toiletries on the slate ledge that make guests smile when they return to their room, well, these are the things that secure me the job, and more importantly, precious time.

At the back of the *mas* are four white stone sheds on the outskirts of farmland, homes for staff who don't have a place to live in town. They're in lieu of a portion of our wages, which I don't mind at all. The fifth shed, painted blue, is the shower room and toilet.

My shed is called Mistral and sits at the edge of a field of sunflowers. Everything I need is in this small room: a bed, a table, a mirror and a lamp. And I learn soon enough that I share the space with an inquisitive lizard, and a feral tomcat that keeps vermin at bay. I still look out for a cough that's more than clearing my throat, or a sore in my mouth that wasn't there the day before, and I still monitor my eyes for recurring blurs, but nothing so far. My eyes are fine, just irritated by the chlorine, and the ulcer in my mouth is from drinking too much peach juice and disappears as soon as I regain my taste for water.

Because of this, I've grown calm. I rise early with the sun, open the shutters and rest my arms on the ledge and let my eyes gaze out onto that shimmering sea of yellow. I sit outside with a small Calor gas stove with a coffeepot boiling on top, and as the morning lightens, I watch the sunflowers lift up their heads and learn to decipher their whisper.

A MONTH HAS PASSED. At night, exhausted after long hours of physical work, I cocoon myself in darkness and heat, barricade myself against mosquitoes that are heartless and ravenous. When I come back from the shower room, I lie naked and damp on the thin white sheet, and listen to the sound of a guitar playing upon the night. The cat nestles around my arm. I like this cat, he's good company and I name him Eric. Sometimes, when holidaymakers sleep, I creep back through the gardens and climb the gate to the pool, and swim backward and forward, proving my wellness. But gently so.

And, some days, I've noticed, I don't check my skin in the mirror, don't check the sheets for the damp outline of my body. Trust that my sweat is merely a response to the ragged heat. My limbs have become brown, and my skin has softened, and my beard grown. I drink in the early morning light and feel content as I begin to launder and iron crisp white sheets.

.   .   .

I WAS GIVEN two days off and decided to take the bus to Arles to catch the Rencontres de la Photographie before September brought it to an end. I got out at the Place Lamartine and to my right was the River Rhône, to my left the site where van Gogh's Yellow House would once have stood—now a nondescript car park and roundabout struggling under the weight of holiday traffic.

I walked through the gateway to the old Roman Town where bars and cafés were preparing for the long hours of feasting ahead. Through the winding back streets, caged birds sang on windowsills under the shade of flowers. I saw a sign for my hotel and tiredness quickened my stride.

I lay on the bed with the shutters open wide. The sounds I heard from the street were comforting—an occasional whine of a moped, the faint corner chat of locals, squeal of swallows. I took out a cold beer from the minibar and held it against my forehead before I opened it.

I woke to twilight and hunger and a ragged thirst. I closed the windows and lit a mosquito coil. I turned the overhead fan on and it purred quietly. I took out a small bottle of Evian from the fridge and poured it over my chest. The movement of air against my skin felt invigorating and cleared my head of the dull haze of afternoon sleep.

I followed the chatter of voices down the road until the incessant hum got louder and the streets busier, and I entered the Place du Forum, and found the world congregating there. Restaurant tables and bars were packed. I found it disorientating, and suddenly wished I had a cigarette, a French one, of course. I went back to the small *tabac* and bought a packet of Gitanes. I stood and smoked. The nicotine made me high and my throat burned, and yet I was grateful for such a stylish prop.

From my vantage point, I could see the café terrace that van Gogh had painted one night. I could see beyond the yellow sprawl of its vulgar commercialism, the vivid proof that the man had once walked across these stones and sat amidst this setting, seeking inspiration or simply company. I followed his footsteps across the square to a small bar with a mute TV and a bull's head hanging from the wall. I sat down at a table by myself. I felt self-conscious and profoundly alone but for that there was no easy cure. I ordered a *pichet* of rosé and a plate of bull stew. I smoked, I wrote. No cure, but it helped.

The following day, I woke early. Outside, terracotta roofs were already baking under the bluest sky and the heat funneled through alleyways when I least expected it to. I constantly sought relief in the cool heart of churches and hidden courtyards where I discovered the work of photographers I'd never heard of. (I made a note of Raymond Depardon.)

By lunchtime, I was becoming agitated by the crowds and couldn't face the battle for a restaurant table, and I bought a bottle of water and a sandwich, and headed out across the main road, to the Roman necropolis of Alyscamps.

There were no queues at the ticket office, and waiting at the entrance were four pilgrims with packs on their backs and shells around their necks. Santiago de Compostela, I learned, was 1,560 kilometers away. Their journey would start one footstep past the gates. It was too momentous not to watch them as they went on their way.

I ate my sandwich in the shade of pine trees, and by the time I got to the church of Saint-Honorat, the rabid sun had chewed hard on my neck. Inside, there was nobody about. Pigeons had taken over the highest ledges and their call echoed in the gloom. Suddenly, a pigeon took flight and startled me. Another launched out, then another, a domino effect of pigeon flight, the sound reverberating against the stone, the swish of feathered shadows, an occasional bird darting out into sunlight. And then silence. The air settled. From outside, the sound of a train rumbling in the distance, the sirocco dance of wind in the trees, the song of the cicadas and a story of transformation.

I suddenly needed to write. I reached down into my rucksack but my notebook wasn't there. I panicked when I couldn't find it. It has become my best friend. My imaginarium. My staff. And I cried. Writing has become my discipline, my comfort. Oh, clever doctor. I see what you were up to, all those months ago.

I didn't stay in Arles that afternoon, I couldn't. I was so affected by the sudden loss and, there, maybe, is a clue to my fragility. I hurried to the station and took the first bus back to Saint-Rémy. The journey felt tedious and overly long and the heat inside felt unbearable. I reached into my rucksack for water and found my notebook there, hidden at the bottom by a fold of fabric. What can I say? I don't think this was about a book.

That afternoon, back at the *mas*, I stood in the middle of my field of sunflowers and faced the sun as they faced the sun. I don't know how long I stayed like that, but when I opened my eyes I saw a young woman watching me from the edge of the field. I recognized her. She and her boyfriend had started working in the restaurant a couple of weeks before. We walked toward each other.

Hello, she said in English with a curl of French at the edge, and she introduced herself. Marion. And that over there is Guillaume. My boyfriend.

Ah, I said. The guitar player.

Here, she said, I've been to the market. A peach in her tanned, outstretched hand.

Thank you, I said.

People here call you Monsieur Triste. Mister Sad. Did you know that?

I smiled. No, I said. I thought they just called me *l'Anglais*.

Yes, that too, she said, and we walked back slowly together toward the white stone sheds.

You looked very peaceful out there, she said.

I was.

What were you doing? she asked.

Thinking about my friend, I said. She had a painting of the *Sunflowers* on her wall, and sometimes, quite suddenly, she'd stop in front of it. Like this. Stare at it. As if she was looking for something. An answer. Something.

What d'you think she was looking for? she said.

I'm not sure, I said, and we walked on.

Acceptance, I said.

How d'you know?

I just do, I said.

Come and join us tonight, she said. Do your writing. You don't have to speak, Monsieur Triste. But you do have to eat. Sardines at eight.

They cooked outside on a small camping stove. At five

to eight, the smell of grilled fish knocked at my door. I opened wine for them, and washed fruit and tomatoes at the tap outside. I sat with them but I didn't write. I preferred to watch the interplay of their kindness, the uncomplicated looks from one to the other. I listened to them sing and strum guitar. I felt the gratitude of a stray dog brought into a family.

When I left she gave me a lilac for my room. The scent is strong.

THE SUMMER is coming to an end. Some rooms stay empty and the restaurant has reduced its menu, and opens only three days a week. People have moved on and my working days are short. I've something that I want to do— to experience—before I leave. Everyone tells me that I must.

I take a taxi out through Mausanne and the Alpilles and the vineyards of Les Baux-de-Provence to the bistro in Paradou. In fading light, I sit outside and drink pastis and smoke a Gitanes and watch people as I always do.

I go in to eat just before eight and take a seat at a table of six. Escargots are placed in front of us, the aroma of garlic rising thickly like mist off a lake. It takes time for us all to look up from our plates, and to acknowledge we are in this experience, together. Wine helps. I pour out Cote du Rhône into my neighbors' glasses. We smile. We make comments about the food in French and English and Spanish, because we're a mix at our table.

Chicken coming now. Salty crunchy skin and tagliatelle with a morel sauce. I don't like dessert but I do like cheese. A wheel comes toward me with every stink of fermentation on it. How long you staying here? I'm asked. Not long, I say, and I surprise myself. I'm going home, I say.

In the taxi back to the *mas*, I feel well fed and well drunk. I look out onto the rugged black landscape, the gold of Les Baux shimmering to my left. I ask the taxi driver to stop and he pulls over to the side of the road. I roll down the window and breathe in the garrigue. I think about home. But, mostly, I think about them. These are my last thoughts, the ones I remember, before I fall asleep.

I LEAVE with the last rays of warmth, as October light creeps in and begins to flatten out the days. Marion and Guillaume wave me off in front of the sheds. I feel them watching me as I walk away. At the gate, I turn back for one last look, one last wave. The clouds pull away and the sun bids me farewell.

On the train, I doze, wake, doze, and I paint the Provençal

landscape in my mind for Dora, one last time. The green complementing the deep blue of the sky, the air fizzing with energy. White stone sheds interrupt the scene, and there beyond the sheds, a glimpse of yellow, shouting. And in the foreground, the quiet shape of two lovers. Always two lovers. Shadowed in memory.

I buy a coffee at the buffet car and a cheese baguette and use most of the change in my pocket to pay for it. I spend time counting out the smaller coins and there are disgruntled murmurs from behind me. They think I don't understand but I do. I thank them in perfect French for their lack of patience and courtesy.

The coffee wakes me up. From then on, I barely take my eyes away from the window. In the reflection, I watch a group of young people sprawling across the seats. I watch two young men sitting opposite one another. Their legs are stretched out and occasionally they brush. A nudge with a foot on the other's thigh. They are boys in the bodies of men, but still boys, still gauche, still unsure. I catch glimpses of my young self in the reflection, as the landscape changes from warmth to cool, from wild to manicured, with gray clouds gathering low around the high-most hills.

I look at these young men, not in envy but in wonder. It is for them now, the beauty of discovery, that endless moonscape of life unfolding.

November 1990

London is gray.

I haven't written for a while because I've been busy.

I've spent the days clearing out my flat until all I'm left with is an armchair and a radio, a small side table—that's all I need. I've a doctor's appointment later today and on the way down I'll call into the estate agent and see about putting the flat on the market or renting it out. I'm making my life simple. My thinking is clear and simple.

I go for a run every afternoon, avoiding the busy hours of lunch or the end of the day when the city is on the move and obstructing the pavements. Along the river is my preferred route, a loop from Southwark Bridge to Hungerford, along to St. Paul's, a struggle up Ludgate Hill, cutting through to Old Bailey and through to Barts. I stop at Barts. Sit on a bench outside and think about G. Taxi drivers sometimes join me and drink a takeaway coffee from the café opposite. They ask me where I've run from and I tell them. They say, I used to be fit, but I've let myself go. I say, You're never too old to start. Some tell me about a relative who died in Barts. If they look kind I tell them about G.

I speak to G's parents, the first time ever. I wanted to make sure they'd received the crate of things I sent to them. They are civil. They thank me but I'm not after thanks. I'm tying up loose ends, that's all. They say they may sell his canvases and easels, I say they should do what's best for them. They say they want to remember him as he was. I say that's a good thing. They ask me how I am. I say, OK. It's a short phone call, but one of truce.

At three a.m., I awake suddenly. And I'm a child standing at the door to Mabel's bedroom. I remember it as the first night I arrived in Oxford and in the darkness my composure had given way to fear.

What should I call you? I said to her.

What's that?

What should I call—

Is that what's bothering you, Michael?

I don't really know you, you see—

Mabel. You know my name is Mabel. You don't have to call me anything else but that, if you don't want to.

She said, We're like a couple of dogs, you and me. And

we'll have to sniff around each other until we're sure of each other. But I love you. And that's a good start. And I'm very glad you're here.

I walked over to the window and pulled back the curtain. Looked out over the churchyard.

Can you see anything? she asked.

No, not really, I said. It's dark. Just trees and snow.

No ghosts tonight? she said.

Are there usually any? I said.

Would that be a comfort?

I think it might, I said. And I was about to turn away when she said, You can get in here, with me, if you want. If you're cold. If the suggestion isn't too silly for a twelve-year-old boy.

And she pulled back the covers, said, You can stay that side and I'll stay over here. And we won't touch. We'll just be company for one another, and company at any age is good.

Oxford

've taken a room a short stroll down from Folly Bridge. It's a fairly large room and I've got my own bathroom. It's more luxurious than I expected, and my landlady, Mrs. Green, isn't nosy or eager to get rid of me during the day. She likes crosswords and reads out clues to me, she likes me being around.

Some days, I see little of the outside world. I sit looking out of the window, peaceful, at ease, this familiar city walking by. I've a cold I can't shift, but I'm not worried. When I've felt weak I've rested.

I've not seen Annie or Ellis yet. Fate hasn't intervened but I suspect Fate is waiting for me. I feel ashamed by my years of silence, but I can't imagine this next chapter and I don't know how to start it. I'll wait a little longer. I need to be strong to face them.

Today, the rains have made the river fat and the towpath muddy. On the opposite bank, a rowing crew is walking back to their boathouse. The wind is keen and is blowing cold, and cloud shadows whip across the Thames. I'm not prepared for this weather. My lack of self-care shocks me at times.

Long Bridges bathing place is up ahead and I'm drawn to it instinctively by the skip of my heart. Been years since I was here and its bleak desertion makes it hard for me to visualize the place as it was, because its gilded memory is one of sunshine and laughter and summer ease. The concrete sides of the swimming areas are still visible, the steps too, disappearing now into the churning brown river water. They've taken away the diving boards, but the changing rooms are still there, boarded up against trespassers. I can almost see myself as a boy.

There was another place I used to go to swim in my twenties where men could sunbathe nude. It was on the River Cherwell and I preferred to go there alone.

Throughout the long winter months, I remained celibate. Focusing on work and working late, and finding my release in grubby magazines I'd get in the post. But from spring onward, I was on perpetual lookout for the first warm days when the river bank would come alive with bodies, young and old.

I'd undress by my towel—slowly, of course—surrounded by students and grizzly dons, and I'd tease them all. I'd swim out to the middle of the river and turn on my back and float, till I knew all eyes were on me. Only then would I come back in, clamber out and dry off in the sun.

I used to be a mystery there. Four summers later, though, had any of those men got together and talked, there would've been little mystery left. I'd been handed around and scrutinized like a well-polished piece of agate. If I felt someone's gaze on me, I'd stare back at them, my confidence crude and shameless. I played with them. A dare was what it was. Your move now, I seemed to be saying. And if they got dressed whilst looking at me, I'd give them a few minutes before I'd follow. I've walked across the quads of Lincoln, Christ's, Brasenose, pretending to borrow books, pretending to study. I looked young then, and my young was audacious. I lay back in those tiny dusty rooms and let the summer dusk unbutton me.

A Rhodes Scholar once. Brooks Brothers shirt and pressed khakis, a man with the premature weight of middle age and a thick, cut cock. His room was like every other room I'd visited. Smelled musty of sleep and spunk and books. We'd hardly got through the door when he handed me a schooner of sherry, hoping, I imagine, to bring a touch of finesse to what we were about to do. On would go the classical music—it came in trends—Shostakovich one day, Beethoven the next, but always the volume up loud. After sherry, he'd encourage me to shower, and when I returned to his room, I was always relieved to see him face-down on the bed, knowing the beast between his legs was coming nowhere near me. And we fucked to the rhythm of strings and timpani under a photograph of a young blonde girlfriend, none the wiser.

He only liked to be fucked, and it was painful for him no matter how tender I'd be, but he never wanted me to stop. I came to realize the pain was necessary for him. It stopped the loving. It stopped the act being unfaithful.

By the end of that summer, I had a serious addiction to fortified wine and a loathing for classical music. London was Donna Summer and vodka. There could be no going back.

I have such fondness for men like him, though. They were my mentors. They showed me how to compartmentalize my life, how to keep things separate, how to pass. And even though they've been, at times, the punch line to my stories or pathetic gossip shared across a pillow, I'm so grateful to them. It was still a world of shyness and fear, and those shared moments were everything: my loneliness masquerading as sexual desire. But it was my humanness that led me to seek, that's all. Led us all to seek. A simple need to belong somewhere.

I walk on. The winds are subsiding. I sit on a bench and watch the rowers train. A child gives me some bread to feed the ducks with and I do so with delight. The child's mother asks if I'm OK. My cough is rasping. I tell her I'm getting better actually, and thank her for the cough sweet. I retie my scarf and walk on.

In those days of my twenties and early thirties, I remember how friendships came and went. I was too critical—a disagreement over a film or politics gave me permission to retreat. Nobody matched Ellis and Annie, and so I convinced myself I needed nobody but them. I was a sailboat at heed to the breeze, circling buoys before heading out to the uncomplicated silence of a calm bay.

Up ahead is the pub where they held their wedding reception. Taxis brought us down here from Holy Trinity, and we walked the towpath in slow procession. The bag I was carrying held towels and swimsuits and when we got to Long Bridges, I said, Fancy a dip? Annie said, You're kidding, right? No, I said, and I unzipped the bag, and she squealed and the bride ran across the grass to swap a white dress for a tangerine costume. Trust you, said Ellis. Trust you to think of everything.

And the three of us swam. Mr. and Mrs. Judd and me. And with hair still wet and dress slightly askew, we drank champagne in the pub garden and ate fish and chips, and the bride and groom cut a simple cake that Mabel had baked the day before. Everything was real, not perfect. And yet that's what had made it so perfect. I said that in the speech. No jokes just memories, a bit soppy really, about how we met a week before Christmas. Advent Annie. How love is crucial to freedom.

In the soft light of evening, as the small gathering became even smaller, Ellis came and found me along this stretch of river. I can still see him, so handsome in his suit, a sort of lopsided handsomeness with his scuffed brogues and red rose buttonhole. And we stood side by side, as light flared off the water, as rowers passed. We shared a cigarette, and in between us was a parched landscape strewn with the bones of abandoned plans only we once knew about. We heard our names shouted along the path. We turned and Annie was running barefoot toward us. Doesn't she look beautiful, I said. I love her. He grinned. Me too. And she loves you. What a mélange we are, I said. It was a relief for us finally to laugh. Annie took the cigarette from my mouth and finished the remaining stub and said, Come to New York with us, Mikey. You've always wanted to go.

Come on! There's still time. Join us tomorrow. Or the next day. But come.

I wanted to scream, Yes, to still be part of you, yes for nothing to change, yes. But I said, I can't. You know I can't. It's your honeymoon. Now go. Get it started.

We waved them off from the pub. Good luck, good luck, have a great time! And more confetti was thrown. Mabel's hand pressed firm to my back, holding me up. It's got cold, she said. Let's go home and get you warm. The gesture almost broke me. We settled silently in the back of a taxi, no talk of the beautiful day or who wore what or who said what. I could see her looking at me. She slipped her hand into mine. Waiting for me to crack. That's how I knew she knew. Had always known. As if she, too, had seen another version of our future orbiting around us. Before its fall to earth on that real and perfect day.

It was Mabel who told me to take the job in London. Come see me at weekends, she said, and I did, without fail. Friday evening, she'd be waiting outside the shop, holding a list of all the things she wanted to talk to me about. And from the restaurant opposite, she'd have bought a bottle of Chianti Ruffino, which would be waiting on the kitchen table, opened. *Breathing*, she liked to say, as if it was a small animal. And sometimes Ell and Annie would be around that table, just like old times, laughter and tears, but with a twist of difference. The pronoun "we" instead of their names, and a newly acknowledged ache that sat in the core of my gut.

Who were we, Ellis, me and Annie? I've tried to explain us many times but I've always failed. We were everything and then we broke. But I broke us. I know that. After Mabel's death, I never came back.

Dusk is falling. Too many cyclists on the towpath for me to relax. I'm cold and I want to go back to Mrs. Green and my room. The lights of Folly Bridge suddenly look beautiful and welcoming.

I'VE SLEPT WELL and have woken up brave and ready. I need to see them now, I know I do. Mrs. Green is pleased that I've finished her full English breakfast for the first time this week. My cough has eased, just a slight clearing of the throat. From the hallway, I ring in and check my answer machine. No new messages from the estate agent, London is leaving me in peace. Mrs. Green is happy for me to stay with her for a few more days. As long as you want, Michael, she says, you're no trouble at all. And her eyes dart to one of the regular guests, a salesman who's just arrived down from Birmingham. She hands me an orange juice before I go out. Freshly squeezed, she tells me, proud of its pedigree.

I set out in autumn sunshine. Through Christ Church meadow to the High Street, a slow amble down to Magdalen Bridge, and The Plain. As I get close to St. Clement's, all I can think about is seeing her again, Ms. Annie Actually, and anxiety begins to overwhelm me, and in my head I'm trying to control how it's going to be, what I'm going to say, how she'll respond, a smile perhaps, maybe we'll fall into each other's arms and I'll apologize—I don't know— but I run through various scenarios by the time I reach her bookshop. I stand to the side and surreptitiously peek through the books in the window to the space inside. I see no one. I open the door. A bell rings. Mabel had a bell above her shop door, too.

I'll be with you in a minute! she shouts from the back. Oh, her voice.

There's a cappuccino left steaming on the desk next to a biographical study of Albert Camus, 1913–1960. I drink it. Strong and sugary, nothing changes. I drink some more and look around. Fiction R–Z is housed in a beautiful tall oak shelf. There's an armchair in an alcove over to the side. She's putting music on. Chet Baker. Nice one, Annie.

Coming! she shouts. Oh, her voice.

And there she is. Comes out from behind the bookshelf

and her blonde hair is tied up and falls down by her cheeks and she wears dungarees over a jumper, and she stops. Her hand on her forehead.

I open my arms out wide and say, O Captain, my Captain!

She says nothing. I put down her coffee. Chet Baker is doing his best to create a mood of love.

You fucking bastard, she says.

I'm an idiot.

And now she smiles. And now she's in my arms.

You smell like you, she says.

And what smell's that? I say.

Betrayal.

I LOOK AFTER the shop as she goes next door to buy me a double macchiato. I sell a copy of *A Year in Provence* and, as soon as she comes back, I tell her excitedly that I did.

Here, she says. Commission, as she gives me the coffee and kisses me on the head.

Dora used to do that to me all the time, I say.

Then it's true, she says. He married his mother.

I open my mouth to say something but she says, Don't speak to me, I just want to look at you. I wouldn't trust anything you said, anyway. She points to my beard. This I like, she says.

We drink our coffees.

We drink one another in. She sighs. She rests her chin in her hands. Her eyes on my beard. Her eyes on my body. Her eyes on my eyes.

You're back, she says. You are, aren't you? For good?

I am.

I'm back, I say.

D'you know—I've got *vongole* for tonight.

I love *vongole*.

I'll make it stretch three ways. We have wine—

—I can bring more.

And I've got spinach to have on the side.

My favorite.

It is, isn't it? she says.

It's as if you knew, I say.

The bell rings as the shop door opens.

Sorry, says an older woman. Am I interrupting?

Not at all, Rose. Come on in. What are you after?

I have a list.

Tell me.

Amongst Women. *Buddha of Suburbia* and that Ingrid Seward's book about Diana.

A good list, says Annie.

So what shall I buy first? says Rose.

Let me confer with my assistant, says Annie. Mikey?

In that order, I say.

I agree, she says.

Amongst Women then, please, says Rose.

ANNIE CLOSES UP the shop for the rest of the day. On the sidewalk outside, I say, Does he hate me?

No, she says. He could never.

We walk hand in hand along Cowley Road and I say this place has changed and she asks me how. I don't know, I say, I just know it has. Maybe it's you, she says. Maybe it is, I say. I'm sure it is, I say. Maybe you've seen too much of the world, she says. Maybe it all just feels too small?

No. It's not small, I say. It's perfect.

Outside Mabel's old shop, we stop.

January 1963. It's snowing heavily and I'm sitting in the back of Mr. Khan's minicab as it crawls along this road. The wipers are battling. He's never seen snow before and he's driving slowly, big eyes full of wonder. There's a rag-and-bone cart in front of us and the horse stops and shits, and Mr. Khan gets out of the car with a shovel and scrapes the dung into a plastic bag.

What are you doing? I ask.

It's for Mrs. Khan, he says. She likes to put it on her rhubarb.

Really? I say. We have custard on ours.

Oh, you funny fun strange boy, he says and pulls up outside this shop. My new life waiting to happen. Mabel is there and she's old, but she's not really, looking back. And I'm lonely and scared, until I see Ellis behind her. The cavalry. And I remember thinking, You're going to be my friend. My best friend.

I remember the car door opened and Mr. Khan said, One prodigal grandson with two suitcases full of books. And I stepped out into the snow. Later, Ellis asked me, Are they really full of books?

Of course he did, Annie laughs. What did you say?

I said, Just the one.

That was the night I had my first glance of Dora. She'd come to pick up Ellis and I was looking down from my bedroom window and caught them as they left the shop. I knocked. She paused by the car and looked up. Bright red lipstick in a white night. She smiled and waved at me with both arms.

We wait for the traffic to slow and we run across the road.

Are you ready? asks Annie.

No, not really, I say.

Come on, she says, and we walk hand in hand up South-field.

The day is surprisingly mild and I'm happy for once. Overwhelmingly so. We stop at the corner of Hill Top Road unseen, and she pulls away from me.

Where are you going? I say.

Give you both time.

Annie?

She doesn't turn. She raises her arm and keeps walking away. I'm alone. Me and the years. My sight drawn to the figure working in front of the garage.

How little he's changed, I think. His sleeves are rolled up, the same tousled hair, same frown wrestling with a dilemma, be it a kitchen shelf, be it love. A radio for company. He places a plank of wood on the workbench. He lifts his hand to the pencil behind his ear and measures—once, twice—before beginning to cut. The sound of a miter saw whining in the air. Sawdust floating. And then silence.

I start to walk across the road, and my footsteps are loud. He looks up now. He's squinting. He's shielding his eyes with his hand, autumn sunlight glinting off windscreens. He grins. He puts down the plank of wood and slowly comes toward me. We meet in the middle.

I've missed you, he says.

In my chest, the sound of an exhausted swallow falling gently to earth.

ELLIS

June 1996, France

He stands, sketching, at the window of his quiet first-floor room. His limbs are an even shade of brown and he has the start of a beard growing. The deep furrows across his forehead have softened, and his hair is longer than it usually is. He's been here six days already, and every day he wonders what took him so long. He wears flip-flops and secondhand khaki shorts, and a pale blue T-shirt that once came from New York. The collar is frayed.

The window is open and the sounds are of cicadas, swallows and occasional footsteps on the path below. Across the grounds at the back of the *mas*, the air is corrugated by the blistering heat. The color of the sky brings back memories that are no longer painful.

He looks at his watch. It's time. He puts down his sketchbook and leaves the room.

The courtyard is deserted. The tables have been cleared of breakfast, and water from a small fountain dribbles noisily into a granite trough. He sits down in the shade of an olive tree and waits.

He hears car tires on gravel, a door slam. A smallish man with gray hair—sixty maybe?—comes toward him smiling, hand outstretched.

Monsieur Judd, he says. I'm sorry I'm late . . .

Ellis stands up and shakes his hand. Monsieur Crillon? Thank you for meeting me.

No, no, please, he says. I'm so sorry about your friend. Of course, I remember Monsieur Triste. He arrived my first summer here. Come.

Ellis follows him into the cool of his office. Monsieur Crillon opens a drawer and says, The sheds are not homes now, but you know, eh?

Yes, of course. I realize, says Ellis.

Monsieur Crillon looks up from the desk. Here, he says. Keys. This is for the main gate. The others—you must try.

ELLIS CROSSES the gardens toward the dark monoliths of cypresses. The key turns easily in the wooden gate, and he makes his way through the scrubby grass, as Michael once did, toward the five stone sheds and field of sunflowers that lie behind. And he thinks about Michael's loneliness, and he thinks about his own. And he thinks his own might be manageable now.

The sign "Mistral" is barely visible on the left-hand shed and he tries three keys before one turns. He pushes hard against the door. An oblique ray of sunlight cuts through the dust and gloom. A lizard scatters across the floor.

You got here then. I knew you'd come.

Nineteen. In his favorite striped Breton top, holding water and peaches. Look out there, Ell.

Ellis goes to the shutters. He pulls them open and the frame fills with sunflowers, a yellow world of beauty stretching as far as the eye can see. He lights a cigarette and leans against the ledge. Swallows soar with heat on their wings.

Did you know you were ill, he thinks. When did you know?

The song of cicadas unrelenting, always there.

I never would have left your side.

He walks out to the middle of the golden field and faces the sun, and he thinks, We did have time. We had so much more than many do.

And he feels all right. And he knows he'll be all right. And that is enough.

. . .

IN THE FRONT BEDROOM, propped up among the books, is a color photograph of three people, a woman and two men. They are tightly framed, their arms around one another, and the world beyond is out of focus, and the world on either side excluded. They look happy, they really do. Not just because they are smiling but because there is something in their eyes, an ease, a joy, something they share. It was taken in spring or summer, you can tell by the clothes they are wearing (T-shirts, pale colors, that sort of thing), and, of course, because of the light.

THE LOCATION of the photograph was not glamorous, not a holiday destination, or a once-in-a-lifetime visit. It was taken in the back garden of Ellis and Annie's house. The photographer wasn't a photographer at all but a wood merchant. He had just delivered the oak floorboards that Ellis had planned to lay in the back room, a job he never got to start. He came into the back garden and music was playing, the three of them sprawled on a blanket on the grass. The woman, Annie, had a camera and she asked him, Would you? And he took the camera from her, and he took his time because he wanted to get them right. He thought they looked so happy, and he thought they were family, and he wanted to show that in the photograph. They were all that mattered on that hot sunny evening in June 1991. And in the fleeting moment in which he met them, he realized that it wasn't the woman, Annie, who held this small group together, but the man with scruffy dark hair. There was something in the way the other two looked at him, and that's why he was in the middle, his arms tightly around them. As if he'd never let them go.

The shutter clicked. The wood merchant knew he had got the photograph and didn't even take another to be sure, because he knew. Sometimes one frame is all it takes.

See you later, said the man to the other two. What are you going to see again? he asked.

Walt Whitman talk, said Annie. You can still come.

Nah, he said. Not my thing.

Love you, they said.

The wood merchant got back in his van pleased with himself. He never told anyone about the people he met or the photo he took, because why should he? It was a moment in time, that's all, shared with strangers.

ACKNOWLEDGMENTS

I would like to thank everyone at Tinder Press for their commitment to this book, especially my editor Leah Woodburn, Vicky Palmer, Barbara Ronan, Katie Brown, Amy Perkins and Yeti Lambregts.

Thank you to Christopher Riopelle and the National Gallery. To the Cowley Car Plant for their generous help, and to the British Library. My thanks to Pam Hibbs for sharing her stories of St. Bart's hospital in the 1980s.

Thank you to my friends who keep me laughing. Thank you, Mum, Si and Sha.

Thank you to my agent Robert Caskie for your belief in this book ten years ago, and for the incredible journey that followed.

Thank you, Patricia Niven, always.